THE BLACKSHIRT
BY
JOHN RIGBY

CHAPTER ONE

Helen Pringle was the most popular girl in the Tennis Club, everybody said so. She was pretty, but not so pretty she'd make other girls jealous, and her smile was a smile for everyone. Most of the other girls thought of Helen not just as a friend, but as their best friend; she was every girl's best friend, whom they'd be sure to ask to be bridesmaid when the time came. And most of the boys would have been her beau if they'd had the chance.

It was curious that, out of all the boys – all the handsome boys, and the ones with good jobs – Helen seemed to favour Tim Leston. Tim was a rabbit at tennis, and, though he'd be a solicitor one day, he was still only an articled clerk with years to go before he'd qualify. It wasn't that he was good-looking either; he was rather small, though he had intelligent eyes, and he looked sharp.

The thing that made Helen tolerate Tim Leston, was that she could rely on him. He was always hanging-around Helen, ready to be a dogsbody for her, and she liked that. Tim was a terrific club man: he'd do anything for the Club, all the thankless tasks. A club needed people like Tim Leston even more than they needed good tennis players – the Club would have collapsed without Tim, and without people like Pat Curry, the girl who nobody noticed but who was always there, smiling behind the teacups and serving the tea. Pat Curry was Helen's best girlfriend; she worshipped Helen, and dogsbodied for her, just like Tim.

It made some of the other men feel uncomfortable, the way Tim made such a thing of his devotion to the Club. They said he was a fanatic, like those fanatics who were dedicated to their Students' Clubs at German Universities like Heidelberg, where they all wore club-caps and sang club songs in a fanatical way. Tim's fanaticism wasn't quite English, people said, and there was something in that. If the Club had been some other sort of Club, one less friendly, then, perhaps, you might not have noticed fanaticism like Tim's. But, as it was, some people were a little disturbed by the way he was always at the Club, and ready to take-on any job, even the most tedious: brushing the courts and so-on. It reminded people of the Hitler Youth in Germany and the way they made such a serious business out of having fun; or of Mussolini's gangs in Italy. Sometimes people thought they'd caught, on Tim's face, the same intense expression they'd seen on Fascist faces on newsreels.

When Tim was offered Solicitor's Articles at Rinkman's he couldn't believe his luck. Nobody could get a job, not even University men, and Tim had only his Higher School Certificate to recommend him. "I like the look of you Mr. Leston" old Rinkman had said "You don't have Jewish connections in your family by any chance?"

Tim, afraid of missing his opportunity, said "My Grandmother's name was Ziegler. But my mother never talks about her."

"It was never comfortable to be Jewish" old Rinkman said "Even in Britain."

"I'm afraid my parents can't afford to pay for my Articles, Sir" Tim admitted – it was standard practice to pay for Articles, and Articled Clerks were usually unpaid. Tim had some idea of asking for a loan; but old Rinkman interrupted him. "Never mind that, my boy," he said "what's a few hundred pounds to me? – And I'll see that you have a little something each week. We'll call it pocket-money."

Young Gerald Rinkman was serving Articles in his father's firm, and, right from the start, he took Tim under his wing.

"The old man has taken a shine to you" said Gerald "There aren't many gentiles that the old-man takes-to."

3

Gerald Rinkman's wealth could so easily have set him apart from the other articled clerks, who could hardly scrape-together a tram fare; while Gerald had a flash sports-car, and plenty of the ready. But Gerald was the most popular man in the office; there was no side to Gerald Rinkman.

Tim and Gerald took to going out for a drink together, at lunchtimes, or after work. It was usually Gerald who suggested it, and he usually paid; though, sometimes, he let Tim pay, so that it wouldn't look like condescension on his part. They'd go to one of the Liverpool city pubs near to the office; a pub with character like the Basnett Bar, or, perhaps, to the bar at the Stork Hotel. The Firm's office was on the first floor of one of the solid blocks on North John Street.

One day, when they were together in the Basnett, Gerald happened to mention that he'd been a keen tennis-player at school, and Tim said "Why not join our Club?"

"Do you accept Jews?" Gerald asked.

The question took Tim by surprise "Why ever not?" he said.

Gerald laughed "If you were a Jew, you'd understand – oh, I know about your grandmother with the convenient name, who might have been Jewish. But, if you were really a Jew..."

Tim said "Does it happen in England? Anti-semitism? – I can't believe it."

Gerald said "Do you know, my Dad was refused by half-a-dozen Golf-Clubs before one accepted him? Liverpool Jews were even talking of starting their own Golf-Club."

"Our tennis-club's not like that!" said Tim indignantly.

"Do you have a single Jewish member?" said Gerald; and then, with a forced laugh, he added "Unless, of course, your grandmother really was a Jew."

Tim paused to think "No" he said – he'd never realised it before "Come to think of it, there aren't any Jews at our Club."

Gerald's only answer to that was a bitter smile, and Tim hastened to re-assure him "Let me propose you for the Club, Gerald. You'll be welcome."

"You may be unpleasantly surprised" Gerald said.

Gerald Rinkman's name came up for membership with three others at the Annual General Meeting of the Club, and the others were all nodded through, unopposed.

"Who's this?" said the Club Chairman "Ikey Moses?"

Everybody laughed, and that made Tim blush with shame and anger. "He's my friend" he said.

"You've got some funny friends" said the Chairman "What's his tennis like? Can he play?"

There was an uncomfortable silence, and Tim feared the worst: that the Chairman would call for a negative vote. Then someone spoke out, and it was Helen Pringle "Aren't they suffering enough in Europe? – The Jews, I mean."

A man shouted from the back of the room "Herr Hitler's got the right idea. The Germans have all got jobs, while we English are all beggars. I blame the Jews."

There was some noise at that, and murmurs of approval. But Helen managed to be heard above the din. "You're a cad; a cruel cad" she shouted. She was nearly crying, when she added "If the Club turns Gerald Rinkman down, I'll resign."

That was something, coming from the most popular girl in the Club, and it got them on her side. "Fair play" they shouted "Good old Helen."

But the vote was close. Gerald Rinkman was elected, but only just.

Afterwards, Tim said "Thanks a million, Helen. Without you, I'd have lost."

"You must think a lot of this Gerald Rinkman" she said.

"He's a good sport" Tim answered "And I owe his

father a favour, for my job."

CHAPTER TWO

It was a perfect afternoon for tennis when Gerald made his first appearance at the Club. It was what they called a Club Saturday, when there were no team matches against other clubs, and everyone who turned-up got a game. Sometimes, if it was wet or windy, hardly anyone turned up, but that afternoon was perfect for tennis, and for watching, and chatting, and drinking tea.

It was a pretty club; there was a lawn in front of the Clubhouse Pavilion with deckchairs, where you could watch the tennis and have tea; and, at the far end, beyond the courts, there was a shrubbery.

Gerald was on court, playing his first game at the Club, and Tim was sitting in a deckchair beside Helen, waiting their turn to go on. Helen had the sort of looks that suited a tennis-frock; the fresh, healthy look, with her fair, slightly bronzed hair, and lightly-bronzed skin to match.

Tim wished he could tell Helen what he felt about her; he wanted to say "Oh, Helen, you do look spiffing!" – something like that; but he felt too tongue-tied. Instead, just for something to say, and not because he was thirsty, he said "I say – how about tea?"

Helen didn't seem to notice, she was so absorbed in watching the game.

Gerald wasn't having it all his own way. It was a men's doubles, and the other men were team players, two from the second VI and one from the first. They had started the game in fun, but now it was serious, and hot work in the sun. Nobody ever bothered to watch the tennis on Club Saturdays; it was just a backdrop to all the socialising. But people were watching this game, no doubt about that. All the girls, especially, were watching, and the four players knew it. They were chasing every return, and going for their shots, as if it was a proper team match. The first-VI player, who was one of Gerald's opponents, began to dispute calls, which was unheard of on Club Saturdays. As befitted a newcomer to the Club, Gerald just smiled and didn't argue; but he played his next shots ruthlessly.

It wasn't only Gerald's tennis that the girls were watching, but his handsome Levantine looks, set-off to such advantage against his tennis whites. He was wearing shorts that were almost too daring, there were so short – most of the older men still sported long bags, like cricket flannels, and, though the younger men mostly wore shorts, they were down-to-the-knee, not like Gerald's. There was a burst of clapping, and Helen joined-in, sitting-up in her deckchair to get a better view. "Oh, good shot!" she called-out – "Wasn't that a good shot, Tim?"

Tim forced himself to applaud; he was beginning to regret ever having introduced Gerald to the Club.

"Gerald Rinkman will get into the first VI," Helen was saying – "Is he as good a lawyer as he is a tennis player, Tim?"

Tim laughed, but there was irony in the laugh. It was the first time Helen had ever noticed bitterness in Tim. "Have you ever heard of a Jewish lawyer who wasn't a good lawyer?" He replied "Jews are clever. Gerald's clever."

"Clever and handsome, and good at games!" Helen said "It's not fair!"

"Not fair?" Tim said "I suppose you mean not fair on me?"

"You're being silly" she said "If Gerald's clever, so are you, Tim. It was clever of you to propose him for the Club."

He said "Wasn't it shocking, how many members opposed Gerald? – There's this awful anti-Jewish thing. Oswald Mosley and his Blackshirts. Goose-stepping about and copying Hitler. And this terrible business in Germany, Helen – smashing-up Jewish shops."

8

Helen said "How on earth could members of this Club have anything against Gerald?"

At that moment, Gerald's opponent hit hard and low, but Gerald sprang to cut the ball off, and to win the set.

"Well played!" everybody shouted, and Helen said "They've forgotten their hostility. Gerald's popular already."

Tim said "Everything comes easy to Gerald – games, money, girls."

Gerald came across; he was sweating. "Hot work!" he said "I enjoyed that."

Tim said "That backhand of yours will get you into the First VI."

"But, first of all" Gerald said "I needed you, Tim, to get me into the Club. I won't forget it – you're next on court, by the way."

Tim went off to join a mixed-doubles on the far court, where they were already knocking-up and waiting for him.

Gerald said "I need a cool drink. Can I get you a drink, Helen?"

She smiled up at him "Thanks Gerald; orangeade, with ice and a straw."

He went across to the trestle table in front of the pavilion. There was a girl behind the teacups who you'd hardly notice; but when Gerald spoke to her she had a nice smile. She blushed when he asked her for the cold drinks.

He came back to Helen with the drinks and said "Do you think Tim will mind if I bag his deckchair? – only until he finishes his set of course." and he added "Some men are as possessive about their deckchairs as they are about their girls."

She laughed "I'm not Tim Leston's possession, by any means." She bent forward to suck the straw, and he thought – she's pretty; and the shape of her lips around the straw made him think he'd like to kiss her.

She glanced up, and, seeing the way he was looking at

her, she said "Sit down, and talk to me."

He sat, and she said "What heaven! – A cool orangeade on a summer's afternoon!"

The deckchair had been adjusted low. Gerald was sitting deep and low in it, with his legs sprawled out in front, and she noticed the hairs on his legs, like black wire. She smiled at him, and he took a long suck on his straw. He said "Yes, it is heaven – I needed that drink. I sweat too much."

His tennis shirt was damp, and, at the open neck, droplets of moisture glinted in the sunshine. She felt a stab of sexuality, and, to cover-up, she pretended to be watching the tennis. Nobody was really bothering to watch since Gerald had come-off court; it was like a field after the predators have gone-away, and the rabbits have come out to play.

Helen said "Tim's lost another game. At this rate, his set won't take long." She was a little ashamed at having a boyfriend who was such a rabbit, when she could have taken her pick of the predators. She said " He doesn't like losing. I keep telling him not to take himself so seriously."

Gerald said "Tim takes his work seriously. You've got to take some things seriously, Helen."

"Work is work, and fun is fun" she said.

"It's a Jewish fault" he replied "Taking everything seriously; even games."

"Tim isn't a Jew" she said.

"Has he told you about his mysterious grandmother?" Gerald said "I was surprised at how my father took to Tim. My father doesn't often take a shine to gentiles."

"Why not?" she asked. But, really, she knew the answer already, after the Club A.G.M.

"If you were a Jew, you wouldn't need to ask that question" Gerald said "My father was turned-down by one golf club after another. I was worried I'd be blackballed here."

"I was ashamed at the Club A.G.M." she said.

"You'll have heard of Oswald Mosley?" he asked. He'd turned-around on the deckchair to face her, and he was no longer sprawling. He was speaking more loudly, and she could tell he was becoming excited; soon he would draw attention to himself. She raised her eyebrows, as a sort of warning signal, and he stopped in mid-sentence. He laughed it off, and said quietly "I know it's boring; but Mosley has two-hundred-thousand followers, Helen! Blackshirts! – the British Union of Fascists. Is it any wonder that I get worked-up?"

She said "You're not at all boring, Gerald. But Mosley's Fascists are just the scum on the surface. People make fun of them."

His comment was bitter: "People in Germany used to make fun of Hitler..."

She said "Tim's finished his set." Tim was shaking hands with his opponents, and with his partner, then he was coming across to join them; and Helen saw that he was trying to smile. She said "Don't look so hot and bothered, Tim. Didn't you enjoy your game?"

Gerald jumped-up from the deckchair – Tim's deckchair – and said "Let me get you a drink, Tim. Orange with ice?"

"No thanks" Tim said abruptly "Who could enjoy losing a set six - love? I made a show of myself."

Helen said "Who cares? – You had some good rallies." But Gerald said "I know just how you feel, Tim. Look, let's put in some practice together; early mornings before work. How about it?"

It was just the offer to raise Tim's spirits. He said "Thanks Gerald. You're a pal."

Helen looked at them both and realised that they understood one another in a way she'd never be able to understand them. There was Tim, all bony and intense, with his tennis shorts cut too long, down to his knees: Tim, who, after each inept shot had tried to concentrate even harder, as though his life depended on it. She said "Both of you take everything too seriously."

Tim said "Now you know, Helen, why I admire Jews."

Gerald said "I'm afraid I have to leave early. Can I give anyone a lift?"

Tim noticed Helen's hesitant look, as if she was wanting to accept, and he was quick to say "Helen and I haven't been on court together yet. But we'll see you tonight at the Club dance."

After Gerald had gone, Helen said reproachfully "Tim, did you have to? – I may never again get the chance of a spin in a sports car."

That annoyed Tim but he tried not to show it. "I'll get a car soon. You'll see." he said. But he knew that he'd never be able to afford a car that had a roar like the car that was driving away.

There was a dance at the tennis club every other Saturday during the Spring and Summer; they were just hops really, quite informal: short frocks and all that, and blazers for the men. The dances were popular, and even people from outside the club wanted to buy tickets, or to be invited as guests. Some people said it was the band that made the dances go so well; it was only a three-piece, but they made enough noise to fill the Club Pavilion. Others said that they should have a gramophone instead, to save money, and that three-and-sixpence for a ticket was a bit steep, especially for the fellows who were out of work, when they had to buy two tickets if they were bringing a girl. But the Club Committee was adamant: the Club dance wouldn't be the same without the band. In any case, the band were just local boys, part-timers, who played for ten-bob each and free beer. But their music was lively and up-to-the-minute. The dances wouldn't have been anything like as popular with a gramophone, and the profit from the dances kept the Club going.

The band was playing "The Music Goes Round and Round" and everyone was on the floor, going round to the music. Helen was dancing with Tim; she never seemed to get a chance to dance with anyone else. In a way it was flattering, to have somebody so obviously devoted to her; but it was irritating too. She looked around at all the couples doing the foxtrot, and at the band in the corner who were enjoying themselves as much as anyone, and making so much sound you had to shout to be heard. The Pavilion wasn't really big enough to hold all those people; but that made it all the more fun.

"Have you seen Gerald?" she shouted down Tim's ear; and then she caught sight of him, as he came through the door. He paused as he caught sight of them, and waved. Then she saw him make the stiff, little bow, that, afterwards, she came to associate with him: the bow that was Gerald Rinkman's idiosyncrasy – a touch of formality with a hint of something continental and flattering; and, perhaps, a little condescending.

The girl to whom Gerald bowed and invited to dance couldn't have been more surprised and pleased. She was the girl who had served him with orangeade that afternoon, but now, she hadn't even her teacups to hide behind. Helen might have been jealous, but the girl was only Pat Curry, and nobody could have been jealous of Pat.

The foxtrot ended, and Gerald thanked Pat with another little bow. The man who played the saxophone and did the vocals announced an interval, and Gerald came across to say hello.

"Hello Helen, hello Tim" he said "Wizard party!"

Tim said "We thought you were never coming," and Gerald said "I'll get some drinks. Beer for me – and for you, Tim? What's yours Helen?"

"Gin and It, please Gerald" she said "With a cherry."

"Gin and It suits you: Helen, the "It" girl" he said, and gave his little bow.

He was incredibly quick, getting the drinks; he seemed to be able to glide through the crush around the bar, without jostling anyone or giving offence. It was something for a girl to admire, and something to irritate Tim.

Helen found herself wanting to dance with Gerald, and hoping he'd ask her. She turned away from Tim, and, looking directly at Gerald, stirred her drink with her cherry-on-a-stick. Then she popped the cherry between her lips and held it there for a second, like a kiss.

The bank struck-up again, and Gerald made his little bow, – not to Helen, but to Tim. "I'd like to ask Helen to dance" he said.

A touch of red came across Tim's face, and the touch of a frown. But he managed to recover himself and to say "Go ahead old man. We're all pals, after all."

It was a slow foxtrot this time, and the music was quieter – it was always quieter after the interval, when it was starting to get dark outside, even in summertime. There was always a late-night mood, after the interval.

So, Helen didn't need to shout, but there was enough sound to stop anyone overhearing. She said "I don't need Tim Leston's approval to dance with someone else."

He could see that she was put-out. He said "I'm sorry" and she felt the pressure of his hand on her back as he led her into a syncopated routine of clever steps. She said, "You're such a good dancer, Gerald! – Is there anything you're not good at?"

He laughed "I told you. We Jews can't do anything without taking it seriously. Even our comedians take themselves seriously."

There was a lot in what he said, and she knew that many Englishmen would not have wanted to appear quite so skilful at ballroom-dancing. It was, well, a bit too flash; not quite British, and just what you might expect of a Jew. Now that she came to think of it, so many of the top dance-band leaders were Jewish.

She felt the strength of his leg as a pivot against her leg, as he guided her around him. She said "Perhaps that's the trouble, Gerald. Perhaps you Jews would be more popular if you weren't so good at things. If, sometimes, you were losers."

He said "Do you think we're unpopular Helen?"

"Who is it who joins the Blackshirts?" she replied "Or Hitler's Brownshirts? – Jealous people, Gerald, that's who."

She looked up at him, and his face was clouded; but, with an effort, he managed to restore the sun. He said "Let's not be gloomy. This is a party; a time for fun."

Helen said "And you make a thorough job of fun, don't you? Like everything else."

"It's the Jewish way" he said "So, let's show everyone that we can dance!"

The band seemed to sense his mood, and though it was time for a break before the next dance, they switched tempo, and went right into a quickstep. It was dancing the way Helen had never danced before; so easy, that she had only to respond to Gerald's lead, and to his quick, confident, movements. People were beginning to notice, and to clear a space for them. They were under the spotlight, encircled by shadowy figures; anonymous shapes. But, for only an instant, she glimpsed, in reflected light, a face tortured by jealousy, and it was Tim's.

The music stopped, and everyone clapped. It might have been embarrassing, but Gerald altered his little bow into one that was self-deprecating. He said "Any chance of another dance later-on? – I don't want to upset Tim. Tim's my pal."

That really annoyed Helen, and she said "I make my own decisions. We flappers do have the vote now, in case you've forgotten."

Tim was early in to the office next day, but Gerald was there before him. "Morning, Tim" Gerald said "The old-man wants to see you."

Old Mr Rinkman said "I want you to go to London, Tim – a few months in our London Agent's office will be good experience. And you won't be out of pocket, I promise you."

Many provincial Law-firms – the go-ahead ones – had a London Agent: an associated firm of Solicitors, within easy distance of the City Law-Courts. Most of the important litigation took-place in London, and an Articled-Clerk with a bright future could expect to spend six-months of his Articles there.

"What did I tell you?" Gerald said, when Tim came out of the old-man's office "The old-man thinks a lot of you."

Tim had mixed feelings: the London Agent's office! – It showed that he would have a future with the firm, after he qualified: the old-man was prepared to invest in him. He knew he should feel grateful and flattered; but there was Helen and the thought of leaving Helen alone with all the other fellows at the Club, and everywhere else. Ever since that first time he'd asked Helen to go out with him, and they'd gone together to the pictures, he'd hardly let another fellow get a look-in. It had been bad enough the previous evening when she'd been dancing with Gerald; but at least he could trust Gerald: Gerald was his pal.

He could see that Gerald was expecting him to be all excited and keen about the move to London, so he said "It's a wonderful opportunity, Gerald. I'm grateful to your father."

"Good show!" Gerald said "I'll stand you a beer at lunchtime, to celebrate."

The Basnett Bar was as crowded as it usually was at lunchtime. It was a pub of awkward angles, full of stools and people's knees, and big shoulders always blocking the bar. But Gerald, using his smile like a talisman, and a scouser joke like a password, found a way through. In Liverpool, if you were known as a sportsman and could hold you own with the wisecracks you were "in". A lot of the men, and the girls too, seemed to know Gerald, and not just the City types either. There was one man with a red face and navvy's hands who might have been a docker; he was looking surly, until he caught sight of Gerald, when his face lit up, and he said, in rhyming scouse "Well, worra' you know; it's Ikey-Mo! – worra' you drinking pal?"

Gerald shook the red paw "Not today Paddy" he said "Another time."

"Who's that?" said Tim, when Gerald got back to him with the beers.

"Just a client" Gerald said "You'll find that our business is built around clients like that."

"You mean criminals?" said Tim.

"Clients" said Gerald "What's the difference?"

Tim took a deep draught from the pint pot. He said "I'm excited about this move to London. But I'm worried about Helen."

"You don't need to worry about Helen" Gerald said, pretending to misunderstand him. "Helen struck me as a girl who can look after herself."

"That's not what I mean" Tim said "She's such a popular girl. I'm worried about the other fellows at the Club."

"Well then" Gerald said "I'll keep an eye on Helen for you. How about that?"

That evening, Tim told Helen his news. He'd hoped she'd be upset about it, but when she said "Oh, Tim! I'll miss you" she didn't look upset at all. Then she said "It's a splendid chance for you, Tim," and he was encouraged by her smile, that seemed to imply that her own aspirations were involved too.

She said "We can write to each other often. And we

17

can make trunk-calls on the telephone. And, perhaps, you'll be able to afford to come home sometimes at the weekend."

He said "I'll ask for a Saturday morning off, now and again. That would make a weekend more worthwhile."

She said "You can't beat an L.M.S. Express-train. It's only five hours from Euston station to Lime-Street."

It was dark at the garden gate, and, when he kissed her goodnight, her response was warm. He walked away with a spring in his step.

CHAPTER THREE

It wasn't until the following Saturday that Helen really missed Tim. It wasn't so much that she was lonely, but she'd got so used to Tim and to his attentions; particularly the way he always called for her to take her to the Club. She found herself wondering whether she'd ever go to the Club at all, without Tim.

The telephone rang "It's Gerald Rinkman – remember me?"

Helen tried to keep the excitement out of her voice "Gerald? How nice! – Have you heard from Tim?"

"I was going to ask you the same question" he replied "Of course, we're in touch in the line of business – I promised Tim I'd keep an eye on you."

She laughed, and he said "You'll be on your way to the Club. I'll collect you."

"Do you know where I live?" she asked.

"Of course" he replied, and she was flattered.

He wasn't long. The car was snarling and growling outside the house, and Gerald was already in his tennis whites at the wheel. He said "Let's be partners for the mixed-doubles."

"You're much too good for me" she said. She'd never been in a sports car before, not one with a long bonnet and a roar like a lioness. Most of the time the car just snarled, but, when Gerald accelerated, she roared.

Helen wasn't a bad player; on occasion she'd even played for the Ladies' Second VI. But it was the same on Court as it had been on the dance floor: with Gerald as her partner she played like a star.

He didn't hog all the winners; far from it. It was just that their opponents found it so hard to return his shots, that he set Helen up for easy winners.

After the set, they dropped into deckchairs, and Helen said "I've never played so well. I've never enjoyed a set as much as that."

He said "I only enjoy it if I'm playing well – it's my Jewishness, you see."

The same beads of perspiration were glinting amongst the hairs on his chest, at his open-neck, and, once again Helen was touched by the sex of it.

He went to fetch tea, and there was the same girl behind the teacups, the girl he'd danced with. She gave him a nice smile, and he said "Hello".

When he got back to Helen, with the tea, he said "That girl who does the teas. I'm not sure we should take advantage of girls like that who serve the teas – or of men like Tim, for that matter, who brush the courts."

Helen said "Pat Curry's such a pal! – It's not really taking advantage, Gerald. Tim can't play tennis like you can. Brushing the courts and serving the teas: it gives people like Tim and Pat a chance to contribute; to be needed by the club."

"I see" he said, "My contribution is to play good tennis, and yours is – to look pretty? and to be the most popular girl in the Club?"

She could see he was teasing, and she said "It's what I like about this Club; it's so chummy. It's not just a tennis club: think of the dances and these teas in the sunshine..."

He said "It's not easy for a Jew to find chums. I'm indebted to Tim for that."

"Tim's indebted to you, too, Gerald. For his job, and, now for this opportunity in London."

He said, "Are you coming to the dance tonight, Helen?"

She'd been wondering if he'd mention the dance, and wondering what she'd say if he did. She said "You'd think I'd be letting Tim down."

Gerald said "I promised Tim I'd keep an eye on you –

remember?"

She smiled at that and he said "I'll take you home now, and I'll pick you up for the dance this evening."

When he called to collect her, he knew she'd made a special effort, with more make-up for the evening and an expensive-looking dress.

They danced one dance after another together: quickstep, foxtrot, and even a rhumba. Gerald was so good at the rhumba, and so Latin, that Helen wanted the band to go on for ever. But the music stopped, and the band-leader announced the interval. The lights went up and couples were ordering drinks and laughing and enjoying themselves.

Gerald said "I'll get some drinks." He didn't ask what Helen wanted, but he was back in no time as if he'd managed to conjure up the drinks like a genie from the crowded bar. She took the drink he gave her, and tried to sip: it was cool, and fruity, but it held a secret. She said "It's making my pulse throb. Like the rhumba."

He said "It's just orangeade and ice; with a shot of rum. And bitters, of course."

"A cocktail!" she said. "You're always up-to-the-minute, Gerald."

They went outside, and there were a few couples on the balcony, talking in murmurs and holding hands. Beyond were the dark, empty courts, and, beyond that again, the deeper darkness of the shrubbery.

Gerald said "You know, I haven't explored the Club's grounds yet."

She said "I don't suppose you've ever had to go hunting for a lost tennis ball in the shrubbery."

He said "Come on, show me!" and took her hand.

The path led through rhododendrons and Helen said "People will notice. There's an old Club joke about couples in the shrubbery."

They came to a wooden building, hardly more than a shed with a crude bench outside it. Helen said "This used to be the Clubhouse years ago; before they built the Pavilion. Now the groundsman keeps his tools here."

They sat down on the bench, and Gerald took her hand. There was a smell of composting leaves, and the far sound of music from the Pavilion. Gerald said "You're such a wizard girl, Helen!" and he pulled her close to him, and kissed her.

She responded to his kiss, and she said "Do you kiss lots of girls, Gerald?"

He laughed "Only if they're very pretty" and he said "I say, I have let Tim down, rather."

She said "We're always worrying about Tim."

He said "Tim's in love with you, Helen."

"I don't know" she said "Perhaps he is. He seems very interested in Daddy, and in Daddy's money."

He said "Money's nice – ask any Jew. But I wouldn't let it influence me."

She said "You've no need. You're rich, Gerald, and handsome too. No wonder all the girls fall for you."

He said "There's no dance here at the Club next Saturday. Let's go for a spin in the car, and dance at a Roadhouse instead."

It was early-afternoon on the following Saturday when Helen heard the lioness roaring at her gate. Gerald didn't switch off the ignition, but stayed sitting in the driver's seat, letting the car growl. It was a cloudless day and warm, but clammy from the haze like chalk-dust, that never clears from Liverpool.

He didn't get out to help her, he just opened the passenger-door from the inside. "Climb in" he shouted "Let's breathe some sea-air in North Wales."

Helen was wearing a blue summer-dress and sandals. She knew she looked nice.

Gerald drove slowly through the Park, and across the tram-tracks into town; accelerating to overtake buses and lorries and the big drays pulled by shire horses. Into London Road with the tyres drumming over the stone setts, then downhill ahead past St. George's Hall, with a glimpse of shipping on the river between buildings. "Ever been through the Mersey Tunnel?" he said.

"Once" she replied. Her father had got a friend to take them through just after it opened, only a short time before. It was still a wonder: as modern as an Odeon Cinema, yet as primitive as the workings of a mine.

Gerald pulled up at a toll-booth and fished for coins, and, in a few minutes they were up again into daylight and into Birkenhead, with the river behind them.

Birkenhead was a tired town: the great dray-horses which they'd passed in Liverpool had given-way to mean nags, with their heads drooping between the shafts of delivery-vans. Even the children in the side-streets were too listless to kick a ball about.

"It's the slump" Gerald said "It's worse than poison."

"Perhaps it will be over soon" Helen replied "Look! ..."

They were passing a pretty village, like one of those model villages you see in toy-shops, with a wishing-well, and Tudor cottages all too new to be true.

"Port-Sunlight village" Gerald said "See that huge building behind? – That's the soap-factory that pays for it all."

"Villages like this could save England from the slump" Helen said.

"Perhaps," Gerald replied. "Do you see that big monument? – That's their War-Memorial. It depends what you believe to be the symbol of the future – the wishing-well, or the War-Memorial."

It was only after they'd passed Queensferry, that Gerald unleashed the car, and she leaped ahead as if she was chasing game across the veldt. Helen saw that the needle was on ninety, and then a hundred. "It's so exciting, Gerald!" she shouted, over the wind "Every girl's dream!"

He glanced across at her, and it was exciting for him too, to see her laughing into the wind, with her hair whipped-away from her face. He pressed the pedal even harder and the lioness charged ahead for the sea.

He pulled up on the sea-front at Llandudno, and, as he switched off the ignition, the car gave a little cough of triumph, as if she'd made her kill. It was blue, here, overhead, and out to sea, and there was no chalky haze; the sun's heat was held in a blue bowl, between the Great Orme and the Little Orme and the horizon.

The beach was quite crowded, and, at the jetty, people were disembarking from a pleasure-steamer: children with spades, and adults with picnic-baskets. The tide was ebbing, and, below the high-water mark there was a stretch of wet shingle. People, with their deckchairs, dogs, and picnics, were all crowded together, on the narrow strip of dry beach, while, at the water's edge, groups of children were splashing and paddling.

"Shoes off!" said Gerald "We've got the wet part of the beach to ourselves!"

While she was taking-off her shoes he went over to a man who was selling Walls' ice-cream from a tricycle with "Stop Me and Buy One" painted on the ice-box. He brought back choc-ices wrapped in silver foil, and they walked together, licking their ices, and with the ice-cold sea licking at their feet.

Gerald said "You can never quite get away from cold in Wales, even on the hottest day." – It was true, for even then, in mid-afternoon, the cliffs of the Great Orme jutting into the sea, cast a shadow on the water like cold steel.

They finished their ices, and Gerald took the foil and

crumpled it, and put the little silver balls into his pocket. He noticed a grain of chocolate that Helen had left behind on her lip, and he was about to mention it, when he was moved by a desire that was both innocent and sensual to taste that chocolate. They were holding hands, and he stopped; then, with a touch of his tongue, he took the chocolate and held it there a second for her to see. She smiled, and he smiled too, as he bent his head to kiss her.

They got back to the car, and he gave her a towel to dry her feet. "You've thought of everything" she said, and she wondered what else he'd planned.

He said "Let's drive around the Orme" and the car set off, with a snarl and a roar.

He stopped above the high cliff at Great Orme's Head, where the wind was sharp, and there was only rock, and sky and sea. He pulled her to him, across the hump of the gearbox, and kissed her hard. He said "Wales is Wild. Up here you can see how wild she is."

Helen said nothing, so he kissed her again, and she felt so wild; as wild as Wales.

The sun was low now, over the sea towards Anglesey, and Gerald said "The Conway Valley is at its loveliest in the evening. There's a Roadhouse, where we can have dinner and dance."

"Oh Gerald!" she protested "I'm not dressed for a dinner-dance."

He laughed "This is summer-holiday country: informal. You look wonderful as you are, Helen."

He drove slowly down the Orme, and along the estuary, with Conway Castle across the water, and the hills all around. Helen said "It's beautiful, Gerald."

"You're beautiful too, Helen" he said "Do you know?"

The Roadhouse was close to the river. There was a lawn looking across water, where people were playing croquet, and drinking from tall glasses. There was a row of cars on the gravel outside the roadhouse, and they were mostly sports cars or open-topped runabouts: young people's cars. Gerald said "We've time for a cocktail before dinner, while we watch the river flow by."

Helen went off to the Ladies' cloakroom while Gerald ordered the cocktails. She took her time, putting on more make-up for the evening, to look her best. She chose darker lipstick and did her eyes. When she rejoined Gerald he said "I told you you were beautiful, Helen. And now you're glamorous as well."

She smiled her pleasure, and sat to watch the croquet, and the few small craft on the river that had ventured this far up from the sea.

Helen sipped her cocktail. She said "This cocktail's more subtle than the one I had at the Club."

"That's because the barman here is more sophisticated" Gerald replied. He liked to show that he knew about cocktails in the way that he knew about cars. "If I ask for a Screwdriver at a bar" he said "I expect a perfect cocktail. If I ask for one at a Garage I expect a perfect tool."

There was still some light left in the day, when they heard piano music from the dining-room. Gerald said "I expect you're hungry. Shall we go into dinner?"

They took a table away from the dance-floor, and Gerald ordered white wine, which was brought in an ice-bucket. The dance-floor wasn't much really; just a space in the middle of the room. There was only a piano, but the pianist was good. Helen said "It's a shame – he's such a good pianist, and no-one's dancing."

Gerald said "That must be my cue to dance."

It was a foxtrot, played slow and soft, as if the pianist was apologising for an intrusion. Gerald put his cheek against Helen's, so they could whisper into each other's ear. He held

Helen close, all the way down, and moved with a minimum movement, to the music.

It had been exciting for Helen, when she'd danced with Gerald at the Club, but this was different altogether. It was so different from dancing with Tim, and she was shocked to realise that she hadn't given Tim a thought all day. The memory of her friendship with Tim was like a Disney Cartoon at the Cinema, when Donald Duck comes before the Big Romance. She glanced at the profile which was pressed so close to hers: a Romantic profile, straight out of Hollywood, like "The Sheik". She whispered in his ear "You're such a heavenly dancer, Gerald. I'm floating on air."

The pianist paused, and someone brought him a glass of beer. Helen and Gerald returned to their table, and, while the pianist was drinking his beer, the waiter served the main course of Welsh lamb with a bitter-sweet sauce. Then the pianist started to make more music, something with a bit of rhythm to it, and a few couples got up to dance.

"Let's wait until we finish this course" Gerald said "More wine?"

"Just a little" she replied. – A girl couldn't afford to disgrace herself, and Helen wasn't used to wine. Hardly anybody ever drank wine, even in restaurants, except for the fast set who went to places like the Ritz in London.

Helen sipped, and, when she looked over her glass, she saw that he was smiling at her. He said "I can't take my eyes off you." He was wondering if he could risk making a suggestion, and what her reaction would be if he asked her to stay the night here, with him. He'd have no trouble with the management: they were discreet, he knew that, and he'd stayed here before with other girls; but those had been easy girls, not like Helen.

He thought better of it. He said "We mustn't stay too late; your father will be worrying."

27

They got up to dance again, and this time he held her very close, so she could feel him, hard, against her. It made her wild, wilder than she'd been up there on the Orme; wilder even than Wales.

He whispered in her ear "I'm jealous of Tim. I don't want to give you up when Tim gets back."

She said "You've no need to worry about Tim Leston."

He said "I can't help worrying. Tim's my pal, and I've let him down."

They sat down again, and the waiter brought coffee. It was very black coffee, poured into small cups from a silver pot. Gerald said "There's nothing like Turkish coffee after a good dinner and wine."

Gerald paid the bill, and they left the dining-room, with the pianist still playing; and they could hear the music coming across the croquet lawn as they sat in the car. Beyond the lawn there was the dark river, and the dark shapes of hills; and, above, there were clouds moving across the moon.

Gerald leant across, to take Helen in his arms. It was awkward, with the gearstick between them, and cramped; but, somehow, it didn't seem to matter. Helen was leaning back, pressed back against the hard seat-back, and his lips were pressed hard, and sweet on her lips. Then, suddenly, he broke away from her, and blurted-out "Oh Helen! – I want you to be my girl. I want you to marry me someday!"

She was shocked, and so glad she could have cried. "Oh Gerald! – I am your girl!" she said.

He started the engine, and switched-on the headlights, and, as the car turned, the twin beams moved over the water and over the little boats at their moorings. Gerald didn't accelerate. The car moved with feline stealth beside the lake, and as she moved, she purred as if she too had fed.

Then, suddenly, Gerald swung her away from the water and into the pass. She sprang forward and her roar reverberated through the black shapes of the hills.

"Isn't it exciting?" Gerald shouted above the wind.

It was as exciting for Helen as blood-lust, in that dark, wild land, with the lioness bounding and twisting at every turn of the road as though to head-off her prey.

Just over the brow, there was a hairpin-bend, and loose stones; and the great cat seemed to be fighting to break away from the road and into the rocks. Helen felt suddenly scared, but Gerald shouted "Don't worry!" and she lost her nervousness. But she couldn't help wondering whether he was really quite as handy with a steering-wheel as he was with a tennis racket.

They were through the pass, now, and into tamer land; amongst lights, and traffic, and factories that were still working even on Saturday after midnight; even during the slump. Then came the river Mersey, and shipyards with a row of cranes against the night sky, and a long moan that could have been the hooter of a factory or the siren of a ship.

It was nearly two o'clock when Gerald pulled-up at Helen's gate, but the lights were still on in the house, "Daddy's waiting up" Helen said "He's always been anxious about me; ever since Mother died."

Gerald said "It's marvellous, the freedom that a car can give you. How about another spin next Saturday? – We could go up to the Lake District."

Helen said "Gerald – we shouldn't!" and he laughed, and said "Why not?"

Because, – she was thinking, – Because everything was going so fast, like a car out of control, and they should apply the brakes. That's what she knew she should say, but today had been such fun, and, anyway, what was the harm?

She looked up at him, and her smile was caught in the light of the street lamp. "Yes" she said "Why not?" Then she remembered "Isn't there a Club dance next Saturday?"

"Who cares about a Club dance?" Gerald said "When we can dance together as we danced tonight?"

CHAPTER FOUR

Tim Leston was excited; he was going home to Liverpool for the first time, and it was all arranged. He hadn't liked to ask for a Saturday morning off too soon, in case they thought he hadn't got his heart in his new work. But, now, he'd been in London for a few weeks, and there had been no bother about his request. He'd never stopped thinking about Helen, all the time he'd been away, and his first thought was to write and let her know, but then he thought NO! – he'd give her a surprise.

He'd been saving-up. It wasn't easy to save even the return fare to Liverpool. In a way he was worse-off than he'd been at home, despite his extra money. It was pay really, in all but name, even though old Rinkman liked to call it pocket-money – it was his way of expressing the paternal feelings he seemed to have towards Tim; as if he sensed something Jewish in Tim, and thought of him as a brother for Gerald. There were Tim's lodgings to pay, two-pounds-ten a week, while at home he'd only been giving his mother thirty bob. His landlady provided breakfast and high-tea, but he had to buy his own lunches: a sandwich or a pie with a cup of tea at a place around the corner from the office. There wasn't much left out of his "pay" of five-pounds-ten a week. But he could count his blessings: most Law firms didn't "pay" their articled clerks at all, so Rinkman's were generous – it made Tim angry to think how unfair people were about Jews, saying Jews were mean, when Rinkman's were so generous. And Gerald Rinkman was such a good pal, the way he'd got his father to give Tim this big chance in London, and the way he'd offered to keep an eye on Helen for Tim. How could there be all this anti-Semitism in London? – It was getting to be as bad as Germany.

It was lunchtime, and Tim was happier than he'd been since he came to London. He'd just been told that he could have a Saturday morning off each month and how pleased they all were with his work. It had been a bit depressing, he had to admit, and lonely at his lodgings, with no Tennis Club, and no Helen; and all the crowds of un-welcoming people in London. But now, he felt sunny, and it was sunny, out in the street. He came down the bare wooden staircase of the office building, creak, creak, and he stood outside the door, deciding which way to go for his pie and cup of tea. Not today! he thought – Today's a good day for a beer.

And then – why did they have to go and spoil things? – a little knot of men were in his way, blocking the pavement and hostile. They were all dressed in black: black shirts and black trousers; and they were carrying piles of newspapers with the title "The Blackshirt". When they saw Tim, coming out of the Rinkman Agent's office, they began to jeer. "Look at Ikey-Mo!" they were shouting "Clear-off Jew!"

"I'm not a Jew, I'm as English as you" Tim said, and he felt like Judas, betraying his pal.

"That's a Jew's office!" yelled the cockney chorus "If we only 'ad 'Itler 'ere we'd 'eave a brick through the winder!"

"'E says 'e's not a Jew!" one of them shouted "So, then 'e's a bloody traitor!"

There was a noise, and a disturbance further down the street, and policemen with truncheons. As Tim's adversaries melted away one of them thrust a copy of the newspaper into Tim's hand "'Ere!" he said "'Ave this on me!"

The threat had passed, for the time-being, but London was not like Liverpool. In Liverpool there was only apathy and hopelessness, with cranes and ships rusting at the docks, and dockers who'd lost the will to fight, waiting around in silent groups for work that would never come. But in London there was menace: the black-shirted Fascist menace and the menace of their Red enemies. In Liverpool the marches were marches of silent protest: hunger marches; but in London it was

Mosley's fighting Blackshirts against the fighting Reds.

Compared to the Blackshirts, the Reds appeared to be no more than an ugly mob, but appearances were deceptive. The violence and riot was often deliberate and orchestrated.

The Red leaders looked to the Kremlin for inspiration and finance, and they could so easily have strutted the stage like Mosley. But the Kremlin wanted Red Revolution to appear to be spontaneous in every country. So the Comintern – the International Communist Committee – spread its poisoned web, and waited like a poisonous Red spider in Moscow.

Where the Blackshirts had discipline, the Reds had uncontrolled riot and angry hatred – the Reds' hatred of Fascism was stronger, even, than the Blackshirts' hatred of jews.

What the Red spider in the Kremlin had really wanted was to trap Britain unsuspecting into Communism. So, at first, the Communists worked through the Constitution, pretending to be respectable members of the Labour Party; and the Labour Party almost fell into the poisoned trap. Then, when the Reds were exposed and expelled from the Labour Party, they turned really vicious, and incited the London mobs with poison more virulent than a tarantula's.

It was ironic that those bitter enemies – the Reds, and Sir Oswald Mosley – should once have been together in the Labour Party. Mosley had even been in a Labour Government. But Mosley's Economic policies were too daring for the Labour Cabinet, and smacked too much of Fascism; so Mosley formed his own Party, the New Party – and the New Party spawned the Blackshirts.

The men in the Rinkman Agent's London office were frightened men, particularly the Jewish clerks who went home each night to the East End, half expecting to find their houses wrecked or burnt, and a black-shirted army waiting there to lynch them – no wonder the Jews sided with the Reds!

Only that April, a few weeks before Tim came to London, ten-thousand Blackshirts had shouted for Oswald Mosley at the Albert Hall and Lord Rothermere had come out in their support through his newspapers, the Daily Mail and the Evening News.

Scum! thought Tim, as he stood there on the pavement – Dirty Fascist Scum! But he couldn't help feeling glad that, despite his obscure grandmother, he was not a Jew.

Determined not to be put off by the Blackshirts, Tim set off for Fleet Street where, besides the newspaper offices, there were several likely pubs. There was a buzz of something happening, and it was a Blackshirt rally, which explained the presence of those Blackshirts outside Tim's office. There were perhaps two-hundred of them here, formed-up in ranks, and they had all made an attempt to dress in uniform. They all wore black shirts, with sleeves neatly rolled-up, and most had black trousers. Tim wondered how they managed in the cold of winter-time because not many of them could have afforded the black tunics of military cut that their officers were wearing.

One thing about them was certainly uniform: they all wore close-cropped hair, and the intense stare of the fanatic. They were drawn-up in line at the side of the street, while a few policemen stood close-by, looking uneasily about them, for fear of trouble. A group of working-men, Reds probably, were watching and hostile.

The Blackshirt leader appeared. There was no need for him to announce himself: for him or against him, the man was unquestionably a leader. Determined, tough, and even more fanatical than his followers; dressed all in black: black cap and tunic; black belt and high black boots, over grey-black cavalry-style britches.

"It's Mosley!" a dozen bystanders exclaimed.

The leader called his Blackshirts to Attention – Sharp! Then he turned them smartly to the Right, and marched them away.

It was as if a black cloud of tension had lifted from Fleet Street.

Tim went into a nearby pub, ordered a beer and a pie, and sat at a table in the corner. He still had the Blackshirt newspaper in his hand.

"Grand Rally at Olympia" it announced "Thursday, June 7th – Don't miss it!" and underneath was a photograph of Sir Oswald Mosley staring into Tim's heart.

Tim finished his pie and pint, and left the pub. "Trouble causers!" he said to himself, and he was about to throw the newspaper away. But there was something about it that he couldn't get out of his mind; something which his subconscious seemed to yearn for – the discipline, perhaps, of the Blackshirts, and the comradeship. And there was something else they had which he envied: a Leader, and a Cause.

It was with a glad heart that Tim boarded his train at Euston Station on Friday evening after work; and it was with a heart gladder still that he went early next afternoon to the Tennis Club. But, as time passed, his gladness faded, for Helen never came. At last, he brought himself to ask where she might be. He asked the person most likely to know, Helen's best girlfriend, the girl behind the teacups, Pat Curry. Pat tried her best to be kind. She said "Helen might have gone for a spin. Gerald Rinkman likes to take a girl for a spin in his car."

But Tim knew that Pat was only being kind. He felt enraged and hurt, all at once; and betrayed, that was the worst thing, betrayed by his girl and by his best pal. He turned away, trying not to show the hurt he felt "The dirty Jew!" he muttered "Judas – the Jew!"

Dangerous thoughts burst out of the dam of his subconscious: thoughts of how so many good men were unemployed, and others, hard-workers like himself, could never hope to earn enough to buy even an Austin-Seven. Yet a Dirty Jew could take his pick of girls, and show-off in a sports car with a roar. He thought of Gerald Rinkman with the roaring sports car; Gerald Rinkman, exploiter of the workers; Gerald Rinkman, the Jew!

He went across to the far side of the farthest court, where it was shaded by the shrubbery and deserted. He sat alone, holding his tennis racquet uselessly in his lap, with his mind half numb and the black tide flowing through it, swift and ugly. He thought about the ranks of Blackshirts in Fleet Street, and his drowning spirit seemed to reach-out towards them, crying out to them for help.

He tried to convince himself that he was only being silly. After all, he reasoned, – why shouldn't Helen have gone with Gerald for a spin? They'll be back soon, he told himself, or, at the latest, they'll be back in time for the dance.

He went back home, to his parents' house, and got dressed in his blazer and Oxford bags. He took care not to get back too early to the Club, but, still, Helen had not arrived. He bought himself a beer at the bar – "Waiting for Helen Pringle are you?" a fellow asked him "She may not be here tonight. She's always out with Gerald Rinkman in his car."

Tim forced a smile, which came out like a grimace. He waited for an hour, but in his heart he knew that Helen wouldn't come.

He didn't sleep, and, next morning, Sunday morning, he knew what he had to do. He wanted to run away, to run back to London; but he knew he couldn't do that. He had to see Helen – he still wanted to see her, oh, how he'd longed to see her all these weeks! She'd written to him – nearly as often as he himself had written. He cursed himself for not warning her he was coming to Liverpool; for wanting to give her a surprise.

Tim knew Mr. Pringle of course, Helen's father. Mr.

Pringle said "Helen? – Didn't she tell you? – She's away for the weekend."

Tim could hardly bring himself to ask his next question, but he forced himself "Do you know if she's gone with friends?"

"She said that a crowd of them from the Tennis Club were all going together" Mr Pringle said "Young Gerald Rinkman called for Helen, in his car."

Tim caught the next train; there was nothing left for him in Liverpool – "A crowd from the Tennis Club all gone away together" is what Mr. Pringle had said – but all the rest of Helen's crowd had been there, at the dance.

It was a slow train; the trains were always slow on Sundays, and Tim spent the whole, bitter journey alone, in an empty compartment. Smoke from the engine wafted in grey tufts past the grey windows, and Tim felt he'd never live in sunlight again. He remembered he still had the newspaper that the Blackshirt bully had thrust into his hand, and, for want of something else to read, he opened it. He read every line of it, and then he read it through again, and it brought a little solace to his pain. "Jews!" he muttered "We've got to save Great Britain from the Jews!" and he noted the date of the forthcoming Blackshirt rally – next Thursday evening June the seventh, at Olympia.

Euston station was almost deserted, except for a knot of men, waiting beyond the ticket barrier. These men were not like all the other groups of men you saw nowadays, waiting aimlessly for jobs that never came. These men stood straight and solid together, and they all wore black shirts. They did nothing, and said nothing; they just watched Tim as he passed-by, with a stare that could have been an insult or a challenge.

Tim stopped, partly through attraction and partly through fear. His instinct was to hurry away but he found himself moving closer. He said "You're Blackshirts aren't

37

you? – Why are you here?"

"To stop Jews coming off the trains" they said "We want no more Jews in London."

"How do I join?" he blurted out "How do I join the Blackshirts?"

They gave him the smile of a comrade, as they thrust their right arms forward in the Fascist salute.

"Next Thursday" they said "Olympia – we'll see you there."

On Wednesday Gerald appeared in the London Agent's office. He was standing at the far side of the general office next to the managing clerk's desk, when he called out "Tim! – I bet you're surprised to see me!"

The shock of seeing Gerald made Tim so angry he was shaking; he was angry and panic-stricken all at once, and he felt like a coward, wanting to run away. He couldn't meet Gerald's eye, and Gerald said "You'll know the local pubs – how about a beer together at lunchtime?"

They went to the Cheshire Cheese in Fleet Street, Doctor Johnson's pub. It was packed-out as usual with newspaper people, and people on the fringe of Fleet Street, and with lawyers too. Gerald got quick service at the bar as he always did, and he took possession of a small table whose occupants were on the point of leaving. There were other people waiting for a table, but nobody seemed to mind, and Tim found himself resenting it, the way Gerald could get everything he wanted, even though he was a Jew.

All Tim wanted to talk about was Helen, but he was tongue-tied and afraid of what he'd hear. So he drank deep to give himself courage, and, while he waited for the beer to have its effect, he said "How are things in Liverpool?"

Gerald pretended to misunderstand, and he said "The slump has really hit the North."

Tim said "There doesn't seem to be any hope, that's the

worst of it. If only people had hope!" He paused, and took another swallow of beer. He felt braver now, and added "In a way, I can see what Oswald Mosley's getting at: State direction of Industry; State borrowing to create jobs."

Gerald's mask of friendship slipped. "Mosley's a Fascist" he shouted "He's anti-Semitic; a friend of Hitler."

"I don't condone that for one minute" said Tim "You know that's true Gerald; you're my pal.... But Hitler's getting results in Germany."

Gerald was really steamed-up now, and his expression carried a warning. He said "If Mosley gets into power, it will mean civil war. The Jews here in London, in the East End, are ready to fight – not like the German Jews."

At last, Tim brought himself to say what he'd been wanting to say all along "I went to Liverpool last weekend, Gerald" – he'd wondered if Gerald already knew, from Helen's father, but, as soon as he spoke, he saw he'd caught Gerald off guard.

Gerald looked uneasy, and tried to make himself sound concerned. He said "Why on earth didn't you let Helen know?"

Tim said "I thought she'd be at the Club. I wanted to give her a surprise."

Gerald started to bluster "I took Helen for a spin, Tim. You asked me to keep an eye on her, remember?"

"Her father said she was away for the weekend" Tim said "With a crowd from the Club, he said"

"That's right" Gerald cut in hastily "A crowd from the Club. That's right." But he couldn't help looking guilty, and Tim knew he was lying. Tim said "All the usual crowd were at the dance..."

Gerald defended himself with a show of anger "I don't know quite what you're insinuating, Tim! If you're insinuating anything about Helen – about me – you're a cad!"

But he still looked shifty. Deceitful Jew! was what Tim was thinking. The word "Jew" had breached the dam between Tim's conscious and unconscious mind. He found himself thinking of the Blackshirts rallying around their Leader, and that they were now his comrades against this Jew. He remembered, too, the group of Blackshirts at Euston Station, who, like Lucifer, had bargained for Tim's soul – here was one Jew they'd not managed to stop coming into London!

Tim wanted to shout "Liar!" but all he said was "You haven't been trying to cut me out with Helen have you Gerald?"

Gerald regained his composure, and his habitual bonhomie that seemed to embrace the world. "I'd never try to cut-out a pal; you know that, Tim. But you've got it all wrong – Helen wants lots of pals, not just one." He paused to let that idea sink-in, and he added "Helen thinks you're too keen, Tim. Too possessive."

The words brought back all the shock and anger, and Tim drained his pint for the courage to say what he had to say. "I can see it all" he shouted "You've been cutting me out – call yourself a pal!" He was sounding hysterical and, even in that noisy pub, people were beginning to notice – "Getting your father to send me to the London Agent's office, out of your way. That was your idea, wasn't it?"

Gerald was uneasy; he knew that there were newspaper reporters all around them: people who could turn any sensation into a scoop. "Don't shout, Tim" he said.

But Tim did shout. He was out of control now, and he didn't care about reporters. "Helen's my girl! – Call yourself a pal! And to think of the strings I had to pull to get you into the Club! – I wish I'd never done it: the first Jew in the Club! – the Fascists are right about Jews."

Gerald too was openly angry and shouting back; no longer nervous about reporters. "Take that back!" he screamed and thumped the table "Or you'll not work for our firm, I promise you."

"You showed-off with your money and your flash car" Tim shouted back at him "She was my girl and you cut me out."

Gerald thumped down his empty glass "If it comes to that, Tim, Helen says you're the one who's after her father's money."

There was enough truth in the thrust to wound, and Tim parried "That's all you Jews can think about! – Money!"

Nearly everyone else in the pub was silent, and enjoying the sensation; and one or two were scribbling in their notebooks. Gerald tried to control his voice "Time to get back to the office, Tim."

"Never!" shouted Tim, without thought for the consequences "Never! – you're a cheat and a liar! I'll never work for a filthy Jew again!"

Gerald said, and his voice was quietly reasonable "You'll regret it, Tim. You'll change your mind when you're out of a job. Remember the slump!"

Slump! – the very word was a threat like an iceberg at sea; a threat to freeze the hottest anger in a man, and Tim paused. Then he whispered "I'll never work for a filthy Jew again. For a false pal who's stolen my girl."

Gerald Rinkman walked away.

Tim sat. He'd nowhere to go, so he sat. Outside the pub, now, there was only the cold sea and the iceberg; cold panic gripped him, and he was about to run, to catch-up with Gerald, and to say he'd changed his mind; to put himself at the mercy of the Jew.

Then, outside in the street, he saw that men were gathering; only a few at first, and then more. The men were blackshirted; single-minded; organised: like a rescue team on ice. Tim went out, into the street, and there was a Blackshirt officer: not Mosley himself, but a man dressed like Mosley; black-capped and uniformed.

"I want to join" Tim said.

The officer stopped, and looked hard at Tim. "Tomorrow night" he said "Olympia."

For the rest of that day Tim could not have felt more abandoned on polar ice than he felt in London. He called on all the Law firms, to ask about articles and jobs. "Sorry" they all said "The slump."

There was no hope for Tim, on the cold ice of the slump, and with his meagre savings, he could not hope to stay for much longer in London. In Liverpool at least his parents would not press him to contribute to his keep.

Tim could have caught a tube or a bus to Olympia, but he decided to walk. It was a normal London evening with people enjoying the summer in the parks. But, as Tim walked further West, there was a sense of something different, with more people, young men mostly, all walking the same way, towards Olympia. Past Kensington Gardens, the pavements became really crowded, and people were walking in the road so that buses were slowing down and honking to get through. The walk wasn't a walk any more, it had become a march, with everyone marching together; more and more Blackshirts all together, with Tim marching with them, and wanting to belong.

"Do you still want to join?" – someone was shouting at him, and it was one of the fellows from behind the ticket barrier at Euston. Did Tim want to join? Oh, yes! yes – more than anything, he wanted to join. "Yes" he shouted and the fellow took his arm, like a comrade.

They were in front of the Stadium now, Olympia; with hard men everywhere: hard men in black shirts, and other men, who were just as hard, in cloth caps and knotted handkerchiefs.

"Reds!" shouted Tim's comrade "We've got a surprise

in store for the Reds!"

There seemed to be policemen everywhere, standing together in close-order in case of trouble. It had been vain for the police to hope that the Reds wouldn't turn-up at Olympia: the Daily Mail and the Evening News had seen to that, with all the publicity they'd given to the rally, and to their support for Oswald Mosley. Mosley wanted a show-down with the Reds, and the Reds, too, were spoiling for a fight. Tim couldn't see any Jews: the Jews were too frightened to be at Olympia, even with the Reds as allies.

The Blackshirts stood tight-together in groups, and some had come armed with staves.
They all had heavy boots – ordinary working boots, – except for the officers who had high boots; and some had banners with the Swastika, or with the Fascist symbol of the bundle of sticks, tied tight. Some even had Mosley's new symbol, the lightning-flash, black-on-red.

The Reds had big boots too, and some had red flags; but mostly they tried to mingle with the crowd and not be noticed when they went inside.

"Stick together!" said Tim's new friend, and they all went into the stadium together, all together like a platoon. Inside, there was noise and crowds of people milling about: what seemed like disorder until you looked closer. In reality, there was discipline at every strategic place in the Stadium, particularly at the exits and entrances, and all around the platform.

Each black-shirted group of men had a central figure, an officer, identifiable by his black cap and tunic; his cavalry boots and leather belt and lightning symbol armband. They all stood watching; ready for anything.

"Those are our stewards" said Tim's comrade, pointing out the uniformed platoons, and he laughed.

The Stadium was crowded-out now, and it was near the

time. There were over twelve thousand people inside – Mosley's men, mostly; or Mosley's enemies. Over two thousand men were in black shirts, and proud of it, and a thousand of these were so-called "stewards" – as organised and as disciplined as an army, and determined to keep order.

About five-hundred anti-Fascists had managed to get inside, and there were still more outside; with nearly eight-hundred policemen outside with them, in case it became a war.

Except for the five-hundred Reds, everyone else inside was a Fascist sympathiser – you could tell that – even the ones who weren't in black shirts. Nearly all the people in the seats, all round the arena, were for Mosley; and in the arena itself, like a praetorian guard around Caesar's platform, standing shoulder to shoulder and facing the crowd, were Mosley's picked men; his Blackshirt stewards.

Those Reds who had managed to get in must have been very brave, or foolhardy; knowing how they were outnumbered by all the black shirts and black boots against them.

Suddenly – he was there! Oswald Mosley, black-uniformed, up on the Platform, with the spotlights on him and his right arm thrust forward in the Fascist salute. All the Blackshirts were standing to attention, and returning their Leader's salute, in what would have been silence, but for the jeers and stamping of the Reds.

"Remove them!" ordered Mosley.

The Blackshirt stewards had been drilled for this, anyone could see that, and they all struck-out with boots and staves.

The Reds were outnumbered, but they didn't run. They were as hard as the Blackshirts, and some of them began to unfurl red flags, and to fight back. It couldn't last long, and, within ten minutes, the last Red had been booted-out of the stadium, or carried-out, bleeding but still fighting-back.

The doors were slammed and guarded, and the hero

stood, again at the Fascist salute, accepting his due acclaim and worship. "Stand together!" was his message – to stand together against the Reds, and against the Jews.

Everyone cheered, and Tim cheered with them.

"Look what Hitler has done for Germany!" Mosley's voice thundered from the loudspeaker "Jobs! – jobs for everyone." He paused while they cheered, then he went on "We need jobs in Britain – we need jobs, not Jews."

Tim joined the cheering, and his cheers were inspired by hatred of the Jew to whom he'd lost not only his job, but his girl.

The most wonderful thing for Tim was the control. Mosley would say a few words, and there would be a roar of support. But, when he held up his arm for silence, it was instantaneous and absolute. Tim had never heard a voice like Mosleys: a voice with Authority, like the voice of God.

One of Tim's new comrades said "I'd follow Mosley anywhere – he was an officer, did you know, and a hero, in the last war."

Tim said "I wish I could believe that Mosley could save Britain – from the slump, I mean." And the comrade replied "If Mosley was in power he'd smash the Reds and the Jews, and give everyone a job; like Hitler in Germany."

"How?" Tim asked.

"Just listen to our Leader... new roads... new Industry..."

It sounded too much like Utopia to be true, but Tim cheered and cheered, with all the Blackshirts, until a lull gave him the chance to ask his comrade "Who'll pay for it all? For the new roads and everything?"

"Who pays in Germany?" the comrade replied "The Jews!"

Mosley was explaining his policy now, in simple terms – he was tood good an orator to make it complicated.

"Industrial expansion" he was saying "Financed by government borrowing... if people have jobs they'll have money to spend on what's produced by Industry..."

It still sounded too simple, and too obvious, so where was the catch?

"It's working in Germany" said the comrade "And it would work in Britain, but for the Reds and the jews."

Mosley finished his speech, to a crescendo of cheers and clapping. He was standing proud on his rostrum, and everybody was returning the Fascist salute. Then the comrades were pouring-out of the stadium into the night; all excited and spoiling for a fight; hoping that the Reds would still be there. But there were only the police, and a sense of anticlimax.

It was even more of an anti-climax when Tim got back home to Liverpool, with no job and no money and no pals; not even any of his new pals, the Blackshirts. The Blackshirts hadn't gained much ground in Liverpool – Liverpool men had lost too much hope, even to put-on a black shirt. It was the Reds who got any support that was going in the North – from the dockers, who'd had no work for years, and from all the sailors on-the-beach. But, mostly, Liverpool men were apathetic; numb, with all their spirit frozen inside them by the slump.

One thing Tim couldn't bring himself to do was to go to the Club, as long as he was out of work. He didn't even tell Helen he was back in Liverpool – her pity would have been worse even than her betrayal. She would know, of course, that he'd lost his job with Rinkman's. Gerald would have given her his own lying, Jewish version of that.

Tim went around all the Liverpool lawyers' offices – except for the Jewish lawyers, of course. "Sorry we can't help" was always the answer "It's the slump."

He started to try for other jobs: with banks; the Cotton-Exchange; anywhere. He was getting desperate – there were no jobs, none at all, and able men were committing suicide, in despair. There were sea-captains who'd never go to sea again in any capacity, let alone command a Bridge.

Then, luck smiled on him. He'd gone into an Estate Agent's office to ask about a job, and there were no jobs, as usual. But, there was a man looking through a sheaf of particulars of houses for sale. The man noticed Tim, and he said "I'm a Chartered Surveyor. I could do with a likely young chap like you, to help me out."

It came like a flash of hope out of a thundercloud – a flash as momentous, for Tim, as the lightning-flash on a Blackshirt uniform.

Tim started work the next Monday at four pounds a week, and his fees paid for him at night-school for his Chartered Surveyor's exams. He liked the work from the start. Every week he set a pound aside from his wages to save for his train fare so that he could join his Blackshirt comrades in London as often as possible.

CHAPTER FIVE

There was one thing that Gerald Rinkman had said about Helen that was true – he'd said it that time when Tim and Gerald, who'd been best-pals, became enemies for ever. Gerald had said that only a cad would make insinuations against Helen: their visit to the Lakes had been as heavenly as Wales, and Gerald knew that Helen loved him. But, when he'd suggested they might share a room, she'd started to cry – how could he ask a nice girl to agree to such a thing? Helen was ecstatic, and her heaven needed no consummation; but that only made Gerald's Levantine blood hotter still.

They became a regular thing, Helen's weekends away with Gerald. Helen wasn't sure that her father believed her, when she told him about the crowd from the Tennis Club who all went away together, but he didn't say anything.

As Gerald said – what was the use of having your youth, and a sports car if you didn't have fun? Anyway, Gerald was always so gentlemanly. After that first time, when he'd made the suggestion and it had made her cry, he was careful not to upset her again. He never tried to take advantage; he never tried to book-in at a hotel under false names, or in the same room, or anything like that. She never stopped thinking about Gerald, and she knew she loved him, and she'd marry him one day.

They usually went to North Wales or to the Lake District; different parts.

It was a few weeks after Gerald got back from London that they went to Bowness, on Lake Windermere. Gerald had got back and told her how strangely poor Tim Leston had behaved. Of course, Daddy had told her that Tim had been to Liverpool and had missed seeing her – what could he expect, coming home all secretive like that, as if he was spying on her? Anyway, she'd had no word from Tim since then, and that was a relief.

The journey North from Liverpool to the Lakes had been slow: even Gerald's lioness had to be kept on the leash. So it was late when Gerald and Helen sat down to dinner, but still midsummer-light.

The dining-room was built-out, almost over the water, and their table was next to the window, looking westwards across the lake, to the mountains. The sun had dropped below the mountains, but the sky was light, so that the lake showed two moods at the same time: on the nearside, the bright side, it was gay, with little boats all attracted to the light like moths, but, on the far side, it was dark and deserted under the hills.

They danced a little and drank wine – wine had become part of their routine. Gerald's places were always close to water: close to a lake, or a river, or the sea. And there were always hills. Every weekend was a surprise for Helen; a fresh adventure, another heaven.

It was night now, over the lake, and the hills were hard-black shapes against the soft-black sky. The saxophone was playing solo, and they danced, slow and close, swaying together to the sound, and saying nothing. Gerald was nuzzling, and touching Helen's neck with his lips. He whispered "I'm in love with you, Helen." She'd been wanting him to say it – he'd not said it since that first time, in North Wales, and she'd been afraid he regretted ever saying it. So it came as a shock, this time; a heavenly shock. She said "Oh, Gerald!" and she felt she wanted to cry.

Gerald said "I love you so much, Helen. Can I come to your room tonight?"

She knew she should say no, but she loved him so much too. She should say no like she'd said no the other time he'd made the suggestion. But it would have spoiled everything. So she said nothing; she just clung to him more tightly, wanting him for ever.

Helen went upstairs, and Gerald gave her time. He expected to find her ready: bathed, and changed and ready for him. But she was sitting in her chair at the window, gazing out.

"I'm nervous, Gerald" she said "I'm sorry."

He went to her, and stood behind her. Then he stooped and kissed her; more in reverence than in passion. He said "It will be like this when we're married, Helen. You know you're safe with me."

She did feel safe – wanted and protected; and she felt she could trust him with her life. But a little touch of memory came unwelcome to her mind; a little touch of fear; a memory of a lioness with a will of her own, nearly breaking away from her master, into rocks. She smiled to think how childish she was being to think of it and she was glad that Gerald couldn't read her mind.

With easy strength he lifted her, and laid her on the bed. Then he took off her shoes for her, so as not to soil the bedclothes, and took off his own shoes. And he lay beside her holding her close. She lay there, quiet, and then she felt him; the urgency in him, and the hardness of him, against her. She knew it was the end of waiting; the end of shyness and of maidenhood. She it was who was on him, she knew not how; over him, with her mouth eager for his mouth; holding him hard to her and saying "Gerald! Gerald!" over and over, and urgently.

He stood up, and aside; and he undressed so she could see him dark and manly. She saw that he was circumcised, and swollen – ready; and standing for her, defiant.

She began too, to undress, turning her back to him in modesty, but he said "I want to see your beauty, Helen. Why be ashamed?"

She laughed at herself and turned to him, to let him gaze; and she was English-cream to his Levant-bronze, and lovely for him.

She said "You won't hurt me Gerald?" – and he was gentle. Then, when the time came to be gentle no more, he was Galahad the conqueror with his sword. While Helen, astonished at herself, was aching for him, begging, and demanding More! Begging him to Thrust! Yes, to thrust the sword, that was hard and precious; the wonderful, hard sword with the velvet touch. The swordsman made his last thrust and the sword jerked, deep within her; and she died the little-death of ecstasy.

He stayed, and they slept. Then, in the depths of the night, she noticed that he was standing by the window, looking out. There was a moon, and the black water of the lake glinted where the moonlight touched. He said "You're awake? – Come and look."

They stood together, naked in the warm dark; close together and motionless, with him hard for her again and ready for her. They stayed like that until a cloud passed over the moon, then he took her hand and led her to the bed.

This time it was even more wonderful than before: longer; long drawn-out, with him kissing her mouth and ears; kissing her breasts and thighs, and saying that he loved her; touching her everywhere with his tongue, until she could wait no longer, and she reached out to hold him and to pull him into her.

They slept again; then, when there was a hint of daylight in the sky, he left her.

Next morning was Sunday morning, and the sun was high when Helen came down to breakfast. Gerald was already at the table, in his blazer and a cravat, reading a Sunday newspaper over his bacon and eggs. She'd noticed that he always had bacon, against the Kosher rules. He liked non-Jewish food, the way he liked non-Jewish girls. He looked up and smiled at her, and she should have been feeling guilty, a "fallen woman", but it was all so nice and English with the homely smell of bacon, and she didn't feel like that at all. Some people were getting up from their tables and saying they'd be late for church. That gave Helen a pang: she always went to Church with Daddy on Sunday mornings. She said "Perhaps I could get to Church in time, if I hurried."

"Church?" Gerald exclaimed "Good Lord!"

Helen laughed "Exactly – Good Lord! That's what I meant. Don't you ever go to your synagogue Gerald?"

Gerald put down his coffee cup. "My synagogue?" he said "That's rich! – No, of course not! Never! – only comic Jews go to synagogue nowadays: Jews with beards and Homburg hats. Besides, it would have been yesterday. Saturday is our Sabbath."

His tone was playful, but his smile was kind, he added "Jewish tradition is important to my father. I did my bar-mitzvah for him." Helen left it at that, and forgot about Church.

Gerald was in a mood to show-off, and to show how the lioness could bound and turn, flat-out on the mountain roads. He powered her around the lakeside and up the Fells which she took without pausing for breath; unlike all the other cars that she left, panting behind her. Upwards and onwards; they came to a pub, high-up on a crag, above forests, and stopped for drinks and sandwiches. They sat outside in the sunshine, looking down through the noonday haze, into silence, and deep into the lakes and valleys.

Gerald said "I want to marry you soon, Helen."

Helen looked at him, and she knew she'd lost her heart to him, with his profile like an eagle, here, in this eerie on a crag.

They dropped down then, out of the sky, and once again Helen felt her heart clutch with fear that the lioness had a will of her own which Gerald couldn't control. She told herself that she was being silly, and soon they were by Coniston water, and the car was purring slowly round the lake. The track ran close to the water, and the trees hung low; and, on the level lane around the lake, the car was tame as a pet lioness on the leash.

Then, they were out of the mountains, with the lakes behind them, and heading South for home. With a full throttled roar the lioness bounded, faster and even faster ahead.

It happened suddenly – the impact! It happened in a blur of speed and surface mud, and a long, long skid – when Helen's eyes met Gerald's and she knew that the lioness really did have a will that Gerald couldn't control. The car died bravely, like a lioness caught in mid-spring by a bullet, full in the chest. She died, and rolled over, into rocks.

Silence.

Later, people came. Gerald heard the clanging bell of the ambulance; he managed to stand-up, and was sick. They were lifting Helen into the ambulance on a stretcher.

CHAPTER SIX

After a week, as soon as she could be moved, Helen was brought to a Hospital in Liverpool; her father insisted on it. The Hospital was run by nuns of a nursing order, and it was a place for healing the soul as well as the body.

Gerald was bruised and shocked, but not seriously injured, and as soon as Helen was allowed visitors, Gerald was the first; the first, at least, after Helen's father, who'd sat up with her all night, after her operation.

Sister Agnes met Gerald when he arrived with his bunch of flowers. "Helen can't wait to see you" she said "But's she's still very weak. You mustn't stay long."

Helen's room was like a chapel, even though it smelled of disinfectant rather than of incense. There was a statue of Saint Theresa, and the bedside table with its carafe of water was like the side table of an altar; and there was a crucifix on the wall above the bed.

Gerald kissed her "Darling Helen" he said "I've brought you flowers."

The nun said "I'll take the flowers. I'll put them in a vase." – It was the conventional excuse for nurses to go out of the room, and to leave lovers alone. The flowers were red roses.

Helen said "Red roses, Gerald!" and Gerald said "You're much prettier than roses, Helen." She did look pretty, like a broken English rose, alone in a rose-bed. She'd put on lipstick and done her eyes; the nun had helped her, and the paleness from her pain lent a spirituality to her beauty.

Gerald said "They wouldn't let me visit," and Helen, near to tears said "Gerald, Darling – I've missed you terribly."

He said "I've missed you, too." – He was hesitating, and afraid to ask about the operation.

She said "Oh, Gerald! The operation – I nearly died."

She turned away from him, and he said, speaking quickly and afraid of what he'd hear "You're going to be all right, Helen?"

She didn't reply, but the look in her eyes reminded him of a dog he'd once owned, that had been injured in an accident, and that must have known, by some instinct, that it would be put-down.

She whispered "Oh, Gerald! I may never walk again! I'll be in a wheelchair."

The sobs came, and the tears mingled with her mascara like the ashes of a penitent.

He spoke desperately "I won't believe it! – I can't believe it; you look so well."

She managed to control herself "I'm determined, Gerald. I'll not give in. I'll walk again." She was trying to smile through the tears, and she said "You won't let me down Gerald? – you will help me?" And, once again, he was reminded of the dog, on its last journey to the vet. There was only a second's hesitation before he replied "Of course I'll help you, darling. You'll walk again."

The nun came in. She'd been outside the door, and it was time. She said "You can visit again tomorrow, Mr Rinkman."

"Until tomorrow" Gerald said; and he kissed Helen, and went away.

But he didn't come tomorrow; nor the next day; nor the next.

It was a fortnight before Tim Leston heard about Helen's accident. He'd never been back to the Club since he'd got back from London, in case he met Helen with Gerald. He didn't know if he'd be able to cope with that: whether his mask would crack, and he'd let himself down. So he stayed away. Besides, his new job was taking up most of his time; what with night-school, and all the studying he had to do in his spare time. To qualify as a Chartered Surveyor was his ambition; so he could earn a decent wage, and not have to lick the boots of Jews like Gerald Rinkman.

He was shocked when he heard about Helen; shocked and angry. But, afterwards, when he thought about the shock and the anger, there was something else; something he hardly understood – was it a sense of opportunity perhaps? No, he could never admit that, even to himself: to admit that Helen's misfortune might be his own opportunity. So he allowed himself a little self deceit. I must visit the poor girl, he told himself – It's the Christian thing to do. And, with a smug afterthought he added – A Christian must always be seen to do more than a Jew.

The nun showed Tim to Helen's room and left him at the door. He knocked and entered; and he could hardly fail to notice her disappointment: like a bright light that is suddenly dimmed. She said "Oh, it's you, Tim."

He said "You were expecting Gerald?"

She was trying to look cheerful, but, suddenly, her face crumpled and she began to cry. She'd been so brave: sitting-up in bed, all made-up, with lipstick; and her hair nice. He wondered if she took all this trouble every day, hoping in vain that every visitor would turn out to be Gerald Rinkman.

The disappointment in her face and voice was terrible – she'd surrendered. "Oh, Tim" she managed to say "Gerald never comes."

Tim didn't miss the opportunity to score. He said "Gerald's a cad – I used to think he was my pal, but he's a cad."

Helen said "You mustn't say that, Tim" But Tim went on "It's bad enough that he smashed you up, Helen. But – ditching you like this! Gerald let us both down, Helen."

She knew he was right, but, against all reason, she said "How dare you say that Tim! – Gerald's busy. He promised he'd never let me down."

Tim checked himself. He knew he could afford to bide

his time. He said "I'll be seeing Gerald at the Club. I'll tell him you're expecting him." – He'd not meant to go to the Club, ever again. But now he knew that he must go.

It was one thing to speak with bravado to Helen, and tell her that he'd see Gerald at the Club; but it was quite another thing actually to pluck-up courage and to go. It was late on Saturday night, Club dance-night, when he managed to force himself. Walking down the street, beside the parked cars, he found himself looking for Gerald's sports car; but, of course, it wasn't there: it was somewhere else, all smashed-up, like Helen. But there was a new sports car at the kerb, twin-sister of the lioness; tawny-brown, like a lioness couchant.

The car sat there looking as cruel as Gerald himself and as complacent, and the callousness of it all fuelled Tim's anger and gave him heart.

He went inside, and Gerald was dancing with a pretty girl. Tim ordered a beer, drained the glass, and ordered another. The man behind the bar said "I haven't seen you in ages, Tim." – It seemed as if the man was trying to say something and couldn't find the words, and what he was wanting to say was about Helen. Tim took his beer, and waited for Gerald to finish his dance.

Gerald led his girl to where they'd left their drinks at a table, and sat down. He looked across the room, and pretended he'd only just noticed Tim, and waved.

Tim made his way across the empty dance floor, and Gerald gave him one of his warm, Levantine smiles. "I thought you were avoiding me" he said.

Tim said "I never expected to speak to you again... If it hadn't been for Helen."

Gerald chose to ignore the subject of Helen. "I was worried about you, Tim" he said "But now I hear you're fixed-up with a job."

"You've no need to worry about me." Tim said "I don't

need help from Jews."

"Still jealous, Tim?" – Gerald was growing angry, but trying to keep cool, for the girl's sake.

Tim sneered – sneering was the way to deal with Jews. He'd learned that at Olympia. He said "You Jews take what you can from people, then you ditch them – like you ditched Helen."

Gerald began to rise, as if to strike Tim, but Tim didn't back-off "You ditched her; literally! You drove her into a ditch. And now, when she's no more use to you, you've ditched her for good. You couldn't control your car, and Helen's suffered."

That was the way to hurt Gerald: to mock at Gerald's car-control was like mocking his manhood.

Gerald lost his temper "I suffered too," he shouted "The car's a write-off. My lovely car."

"What's a car to you?" Tim sneered "You smash up a car, and you smash up a girl – you've got another car; and another girl."

The girl was looking nervous and fidgeting with her drink. The band started-up and she plucked at Gerald's sleeve, to dance. Tim said "A new car outside, and a new girl in your arms, Gerald. Are you taking the new girl out for a spin in your car?"

The girl was agitated, and trying to pull Gerald away. Tim raised his voice "You'll make use of anyone won't you? – Never trust a Jew!"

Gerald was shouting back now, and everyone was listening, over the music. Everyone had stopped dancing. "Fascist!" Gerald shouted "You're as bad as those Blackshirts in London. Next thing you'll be a Blackshirt too."

Tim was screaming back at him "I have joined the Blackshirts; the British Union of Fascists: Mosley's men. How do you like that, Jew?"

Gerald's glance was darting now, testing out the people in the room: testing their support. He looked uneasy, and, though he spoke his words to Tim he was addressing everyone. "We British Jews won't lie down and die" he said "Not like German Jews. Your precious Mosley will get a bloody nose if he tries his bullying in the East End. London Jews know how to fight dirty – dirtier even than the Blackshirts."

He paused, and looked around again for support, but the facial expressions he saw were neutral, like the faces of the people in the Bible, who passed-by on the other side. He said "Come outside then, Tim. I'll show you how a Jew can fight." The girl was hanging-on to his arm, and trying to restrain him.

Tim laughed "It's not only me you'll be fighting. I'll bet I'm not the only fellow in this Club with a black shirt in his wardrobe."

Gerald's eyes darted, and there were a few men who'd left their girls, and were edging towards him.

Tim laughed again, in triumph; and he thrust his arm forward in the Fascist salute. "Sieg Heil!" he shouted, and clicked his heels.

"Sieg Heil!" came the echo from other voices, and other arms were thrust out. Everyone in the room was tense and expecting trouble, while the band played on.

Gerald looked in vain for allies, but his old, loyal, ally, had been abandoned in a ditch. "I'm leaving" he said to the girl "Will you come?"

She hesitated and then allowed herself to be led outside. At that moment the music stopped and the sound that followed Gerald and the girl was like the sound of hyenas; the sound of mockery and hate. "Jew lover!" Tim screamed out after the girl. "Do you know what happens to Jew-loving girls in Germany?"

The new lioness moved from couchant to rampant in one great spring, and leapt away with a roar to drown the laughter of hyenas.

The girl was all tensed-up in the passenger seat "Please, Gerald" she cried out in fear "I don't want to end up in a ditch like Helen Pringle."

He ignored her and accelerated faster, as if the city streets were the open road. In the Club he'd felt alone and impotent, in the face of Tim who'd dared to mock his mastery of a car. But now he had the power to make a girl cringe with fear, and to drown the laughter of hyenas with a roar.

CHAPTER SEVEN

Tim did not immediately pay another visit to Helen in hospital. Not that he didn't want to visit; but he forced his mind to conquer his heart.

He knew that Gerald would never visit, and, sooner or later, Helen would have to face that fact. She'd be lonely and vulnerable – vulnerable to anybody who'd be kind to her.

He was right. Helen's pain and despair at her injuries were hardly greater than her despair at Gerald's treachery. Through the slow, long hours her depression turned to hatred of Gerald, and her tears turned to acid.

At last, Tim went to visit, and this time Helen was glad to see him. She said "Oh, Tim! It's been ages!"

He handed her his offering of flowers, and he said "Has nobody else been to visit?"

"Oh, yes" she said "Daddy, of course, and lots of girlfriends; especially Pat Curry."

He came right to the point "And Gerald?" he asked. She caught her breath, as if she was choking, and unable to speak. "Don't ever talk to me about Gerald Rinkman!" she said "I hate him."

Tim turned the knife "Gerald's like all Jews. I'm beginning to hate all Jews."

Helen wasn't ready to agree to that; not yet. Her spite against Gerald was not yet sharp enough for her to stab-out at all Jews. She said "You mustn't say such things. The poor Jews in Germany are suffering terribly."

Tim said "It was a Jew that made you suffer, Helen." He pressed the point of the blade "Why is Germany doing so well, while the rest of the world is in a slump? – Hitler's putting the Jews in their place, that's why." He gave a hyena-laugh "In Germany, the Jew's place is no place at all! – Sir Oswald Mosley's my man. I've joined his Blackshirts. The

British Union of Fascists."

Helen was still not ready to stab-out, and her first reaction was a nervous giggle. "Oh Tim" she said "I bet you look funny in your black shirt."

Tim didn't smile; he was never a man to smile at himself. His face took on the intense stare of the fanatic, and if anyone had described it as a look like Herr Hitler's, Tim would have been flattered. He said "I'm proud to wear a black shirt, Helen. If I can raise some recruits in Liverpool I may even become a leader: an officer. A leader in high boots, and an officer's cap."

Helen said "There aren't many Blackshirts in Liverpool."

"There are plenty in Manchester" he replied "When Mosley came to Manchester, to the Free-Trade Hall, it was packed."

Helen was beginning to think. She ached for Gerald, though now, of course, she hated him; she'd decided that. She'd decided to hate him; it was better to hate than to ache. As a crippled girl, she couldn't afford to be choosy, and, well, if she couldn't have Gerald... she'd got along perfectly well, making-do with Tim before Gerald came on the scene. Of course, compared with Gerald, Tim was rather insignificant, a rabbit, there was no getting away from that. But – a Tim Leston in high boots and a black cap? A Blackshirt officer in exchange for a dirty Jew? – There! she'd said it, if only to herself: a dirty Jew! And all her pain was encapsulated in those words.

Tim was looking taller somehow, and prouder, with his narrow chest stuck out, and his shoulders back. He was saying "I feel full of confidence, Helen; for the first time in my life. There are two-hundred-thousand fellows like me, remember: Mosley's army, and we all worship him. The British Union of Fascists – we're going to save Great Britain from Gerald Rinkman and the Jews." He was talking very quickly now and ranting; and, when she tried to protest, he just went on "We'll save Britain from the sort of Jews who'd nearly kill a girl, and then ditch her."

Helen managed to break-in "You'd never do a thing like that, would you Tim? You'd never ditch a girl who's down on her luck?"

He clicked his heels, and stood to attention, as if he was taking an oath. "Never!" he exclaimed "I swear." He looked ludicrous, but Helen knew she'd have to take him seriously – she couldn't risk losing the only man who'd swear never to ditch a crippled girl. So she opened her eyes wide, and gazed at him adoringly. She said "High boots and a black cap – I could admire a man dressed like that, Tim."

She felt a curious tingle of lust as she said it; the sort of tingle that nice girls never have. At the same moment she felt the velvet touch of memory – a memory that was her secret, and must be her secret always: the memory of a night spent in heaven, beside a lake.

There was a knock at the door, and it was the nun come to serve tea. She smiled at Helen, and said "You look so much better, dear. You'll be going home soon."

The nun put the tray on the bedside table, and, when she'd gone Helen said "Home!" and then she whispered "I'll be in a wheelchair, Tim. I'll never walk again."

Tim looked down into his teacup, not wanting to meet her eye. Helen's words were worse than the worst that he'd been expecting. And yet, he was thinking he'd never have held onto the old Helen, and half of Helen was better than none at all. He said "Cheer up! I'll get a little car – I'll save up and get a car. I'll drive you around, Helen. On my Blackshirt honour!"

She said "You can't afford a car, Tim. You've been out of work."

He said "I'm lucky – I'm even being paid while I'm training. A Chartered Surveyor can earn good fees."

She said "It will be years before you've saved for a car, Tim" and, after a pause, she added "I'll ask Daddy. – He'll buy me a car for you to drive. Daddy will do anything for me, Tim."

He stood-up to leave, and it gave him a sort of perverse pleasure to see how disappointed she was. "You're not leaving so soon?" she asked.

"Duty!" he announced "I've a meeting tonight. A few fellows from the Club are interested in joining the Blackshirts." He was enthusiastic "In a few months it won't only be meetings. It will be rallies here in Liverpool. You'll see."

He turned to go, and his about turn was almost military.

She said "Come again soon, Tim. Come often. And, when I get home, Tim – come to see me every day."

He said "I won't be able to come if I'm on duty, Helen. Most of the big rallies are in London at weekends. If I'm to be a leader – if I'm to be in the front line, I'll have to go to the rallies."

She said "What about the train fares?" and he said "I'll find the money. It's a priority."

"Tim!" she said "I'm dying to see you in your black shirt. I do hope you get to be an officer, in high boots."

He said "Are you a Fascist supporter, Helen?" and she said "I hate Jews!"

He stopped at the door, to wave goodbye, but what he gave her was not a wave, but a Fascist salute.

When, after a week, Tim called at Helen's home, there was a little car on the drive, a brand-new Morris runabout. Mr. Pringle answered the door. He said "I'm glad to see you, Tim. Helen will be very glad. Come in."

It was a big house; far too big for two people. The house had two faces like Janus: one face looked-out at the street, and away from the sun, and that was a closed face, hidden behind curtains; while the other face, at the back, was an open face onto the garden and the open view beyond.

The rooms were large and high; at the front there were always curtains, but, at the back, the curtains were never drawn, even at night.

Mr. Pringle opened the door into the back-facing room. The Victorian furniture had been moved, to clear a space, and, in front of the open French-window, there was a new wheelchair and in it, Helen, with her face lit-up in welcome, like the sun.

It was like no wheelchair that Tim had ever seen, and Mr. Pringle was bursting for him to notice it. It had been Mr. Pringle's big surprise for Helen, when she came home – that and the car. The new car and the new wheelchair went together; the one dependent on the other.

"Take a good look at the wheelchair, Tim" Mr. Pringle said "It's a new American model. It folds-up, can you believe? – Small enough to fit into a car-boot." He was all-excited, and delighted to have been able to do something – anything – for Helen; something – anything – to take her mind, and his own mind, off the tragedy they would both have to face for ever.

"Trust the Americans!" he was saying "The Americans were the first to make cars affordable, and, now here's a chance of freedom for cripples... An American called Jennings designed the prototype for his crippled friend... they formed a Company, Everest and Jennings."

Tim said "It's a wonderful wheelchair, It will make all the difference, for Helen. For Helen, it will mean freedom." He was thinking how, to be free, Helen also needed the car, and himself to drive it. It gave him a feeling of power, to have control over Helen's freedom.

Mr. Pringle left them alone, and Helen said "I've missed you, Tim."

He said "I've been so busy, with my job, and with

night-school; and with my political work."

She said "Did you see the new car, Tim? – Daddy bought it for me. I told him you'd promised to drive."

What a piece of luck! he was thinking to himself – He'd never have had the chance of a new car, not for years. He said "There's no time like the present, Helen. Shall I take you for a spin?"

She called out for her father, and between them, Tim and Mr. Pringle managed to get Helen into the car. It was the chance for Mr. Pringle to fold-up the wheelchair and to demonstrate how easy it was. "Will you come with us, Sir?" Tim said "After all, it is your car."

"It's Helen's car," Mr. Pringle replied "I'll not come with you. I've never liked cars."

Tim set-off, and the little Morris was easy; not like the brutes which Tim was used to driving when he got a chance to drive, which wasn't often. He said "We can't go far today, Helen. I've a meeting this evening."

"Blackshirts?" she asked.

"The British Union" he said "We're a serious political party."

"Let's go where there's a bit of life" she said "I'm sick of loneliness. I'm sick of being shut-up."

He said "We've time to go as far as Southport today. Perhaps we'll go to Blackpool next Sunday."

"Southport and Blackpool" she said "That's what I want, Tim. Places that are full of life. Not anywhere empty, like Wales."

They were in Southport quite quickly, and driving along Lord Street, and onto the front, where there were people and a wide, flat beach, and a wide, flat sea beyond it. There were cars parked on the beach, and ice-cream vans, and a cart with a horse between the shafts. The horse was blinkered and unkempt, with shaggy fetlocks still damp from the sea; on the cart, there was a clumsy set of scales and some small, flat fish that had been taken from the flat, shallow sea. Occasionally the horse gave a tired shake of its head, or a flick of its tail to rid itself of sandflies; while the fishwife, thickly-shawled despite the warm afternoon, weighed-out the fish, and wrapped it in newspaper.

Tim drove onto the sand and stopped.

Helen said "Let's open all the doors."

Tim got out, and opened all the doors, and Helen put her face up to the sun, and breathed the air. She said "Oh, Tim! – If only I could walk again! – If only I could go down to the sea!"

He said "I could push you down to the sea in your chair."

The wheelchair was in the car-boot, folded-up. It had folded nice and easy: it was the best wheelchair Mr. Pringle could buy.

Helen said "Do you think you could manage it? – I wish Daddy was with us, to help."

Tim was determined to manage. Ever since he'd become a Blackshirt he'd been determined, and Helen had noticed the change in him. Tim got out, and took the wheelchair out of the boot, and unfolded it. He pushed it round so it was at the open passenger-door, jammed close, "Put your arms around my neck and hold tight" he said.

She was a dead-weight, but her grip had the force of panic, like the frantic grip of a non-swimmer around the neck of a lifeguard. Tim stumbled and almost fell, but he recovered. He'd not have managed it in the days when he'd been a rabbit at the tennis club. There! – Helen was settled in the chair, and the sand was so compacted, Tim found he could push her quite easily. They went towards the sea, and it was a long way, a quarter of a mile perhaps; but, when they got near, and the sand became wet, they stopped in case the wheels sank. They could see the little waves, that were hardly more than ripples on the water, and the children splashing each other with excited cries. And they could see the sun, through the haze which never really lifts from the Irish Sea.

This was a major shipping-lane into Liverpool, and on the horizon, there were distant silhouettes of vessels, and smudges of smoke. Tim said "If only we'd brought binoculars!" and it reminded Helen of Gerald's expensive binoculars, and the view from the Great Orme, and the view across Windermere. And, for a while she couldn't speak.

Then she bucked-up, and said "Daddy will buy me some binoculars" and then she said "Oh Tim! – you can't imagine what it means to me to be here; to be free!"

"Free?" he asked.

"Being a cripple is like being a prisoner" she replied "But now, for this afternoon, I'm free." She looked out for a long moment, out to sea, and she whispered "I'm so grateful to you, Tim. I depend on you."

Her words and her expression touched his heart, and he felt a number of emotions: sympathy and affection; but the strongest emotion he felt was power that she was so dependant on him. He said "We'll have to be getting back for my meeting."

She tried to conceal her disappointment, but again he felt a sense of power that she had to go with him, at his bidding; she had no choice.

They left the flat Lancashire countryside behind them, and passed a long row of flat-roofed modern houses; then came Aintree racecourse and poor houses of smoke-blackened brick; then Walton Gaol and Walton Hospital.

Helen said "It's so depressing, Tim. Liverpool wasn't like this before the slump."

"It's all the Jews' fault" Tim said "Jews like Gerald Rinkman."

"You must stop saying those things!" she said. She could not fail to notice his obsessive expression, and the vindictive way he stabbed down on the accelerator pedal when he said "Jews!"

He ignored her, and he was almost shouting "All this part of Liverpool – Bootle; Walton – it used to be prosperous. It may not have been pretty, but there were jobs. Look at those cranes!" – He pointed down the hill to the river Mersey "Those cranes were always working; not rusting-idle. The dockers had jobs."

She said "It's terrible, Tim!"

He was really shouting now, and driving too fast. "I'm frightened" she screamed "Please Tim!" – She needed a man she could trust to control a car. He slowed down and said "I'm sorry Helen. Of course you're nervous, after the way you were driven into a ditch by a Jew."

He managed to control himself, and to control the car, and he said "What's the government doing? They call themselves the National Government! But only Mosley could save Britain. Only the British Union can save Britain from the Jews!"

Helen sat silent, and then she whispered "You've saved me, Tim. You've saved me from a Jew."

Tim said "Perhaps you can understand why I've joined the Blackshirts? – Why I've got to go to London for the Blackshirt rallies?"

The Blackshirt meeting that evening was at Harry's house; Harry was one of the men who'd stepped forward to support Tim against Gerald, that night, at the Club. He was big and blond and he might have come straight off one of the travel posters advertising the next Olympic games in Berlin. The newspapers and the newsreels were already full of the Olympics, and of the stadium that Hitler was having built in Berlin; and the way the German master-race was going to show-up the Jews and the Blacks. It was the ambition of every Blackshirt to see Hitler's blond-haired Aryans smash the Jews.

It was a disappointment for Tim that the British Union was so small in Liverpool. Nobody in Liverpool seemed to take the Blackshirts seriously, not like in London. Still, there were compensations: Tim soon became a leader, an officer, and he wouldn't have got to be an officer so quickly in London. He was entitled to wear high boots and an officer's cap, while the men in the ranks just wore black shirts and kept their heads bare. He'd never yet dared to go out in his black shirt in Liverpool, but, when he went away to rallies in London, or to Manchester – wherever Mosley was making a speech – then, he always wore his black shirt, and was the proudest he'd ever been in his life.

Tim never missed a rally if he could help it, and he was away at least once a month. In Liverpool, in the Surveyor's office, Tim was a nobody; but, in his high boots and his black cap he was more than a somebody; he was an officer of the British Union.

When he went away, to a rally, some of the other men from Liverpool usually went with him. At rallies they were no longer a Liverpool joke; they were a Liverpool contingent of the British Union, and Tim was their leader.

That's how it went, for all that Autumn and Winter, with Tim always around at Helen's house, except when he was away at Blackshirt rallies.

The next April, Tim went to Leicester, where Mosley made his famous anti-Jewish speech. After that, Mosley concentrated his efforts against the Jews of London's East End, and Tim was in London every other weekend. There were always Blackshirt pals who'd put him up for a night; who'd do anything to help an officer of the British Union. In London, Tim was somebody to be respected and admired; someone who was always ready to have a smack at the Jews. All his life Tim had had to force himself to smile, while fellows like Gerald Rinkman got all the admiration.

"Discipline" was Mosley's motto. "Discipline!" he thundered before every inspection – the Blackshirts were Mosley's private army of storm-troopers, who were disciplined to stand to attention under his gaze, and to march in disciplined ranks like Hitler's S.S. They never openly instigated violence, but, by their very presence, they incited violence in others and welcomed it. Tim had never forgotten the thrill of Olympia when the mob of Reds had been smashed by Discipline in a black shirt.

The tactics were always the same: a time and place were arranged, and the Blackshirts would gather together; usually on a Sunday, about noon. Mosley would make a speech; as much for the newspapers and newsreels, as for his own men. Then, they would march, proud and disciplined, through the East End of London, with the Reds and the Jews, like a pack of jackals, snapping and snarling behind.

To say that Tim never wore his uniform in Liverpool was not strictly true. He wore it at meetings, indoors; but he also wore it for Helen, sometimes, when they were alone. The uniform never failed to excite Helen's admiration, or it may even have been something stronger than admiration. It gave Tim a sense of manliness to be admired like that, for the first time in his life. As for Helen's life, Tim's visits had become her most important thing. She counted the days and the hours, and, if he ever telephoned to say he couldn't come after all, it made her cry. "Duty" he would say: it was always duty. But, when he 'phoned, to say he couldn't come, Helen found herself hating, not the Blackshirts who were keeping him away from her, but the Jews – there would have been no need for Blackshirts without the Jews.

As for Helen's father, Mr. Pringle, who used to despise Tim, and hadn't bothered to conceal it – well, the change in Mr.

Pringle was pathetic, but infinitely satisfying for Tim. Now, whenever Tim came to visit, Mr. Pringle was down the path to welcome him. Tim had his own set of car keys, and often he'd take the car home with him; and he liked to see the envious glances of the neighbours, when he parked the car outside his parents' house. Often it was the only car in the street; but, if there were any others, they were always old and shabby, with sagging springs; like old men in old armchairs.

Mr. Pringle needed Tim now, that was what had made him change. Mr. Pringle was no longer dismissive, and now it was Tim who'd become the dismissive one. An officer of the British Union knew how to put people in their place; Mr. Pringle was in Tim's power, and Tim never let him forget it.

It was nearly a year before Tim proposed to Helen – well, it wasn't exactly a proposal; when he rather condescendingly announced his intention of marrying her. After all, he knew that Helen was in no position to be choosy and to refuse.

Tim had pushed her into the garden, in her wheelchair, and he said "I'll leave you alone for a minute. I want a word with your father. I'm going to ask him for your hand in marriage." It was formal, and old-fashioned, but that was what he'd planned.

"Oh!" Helen said, in a small voice "You're so good to me Tim."

He said "I want you to walk again, Helen. I want you to walk with me, back down the aisle."

She gave a nervous sob "You know I can't, Tim – Oh, how I wish I could! It may be years before I can walk, perhaps never."

Tim's expression altered, to that obstinate and slightly mad look he sometimes had, particularly when he got onto the subject of Jews, or when he was being an obstinate Blackshirt. He stood-up straight and almost shouted, as though he was issuing an order. "You will walk!" he announced "I insist on it!" and he gave her the Fascist salute.

He fetched the suitcase he'd left in the hall; then he went to the cloakroom and changed into his uniform. He'd planned it all. Then he knocked at Mr. Pringle's study door, and marched in.

The old man was startled, and uncertain at first. "Sit down, my boy" he said.

But Tim remained standing. He clicked his heels like a Junker and said "Sir – I request your daughter's hand in marriage."

A year ago, Mr. Pringle would have found it laughable, but now he was in no position to laugh. The slightly glazed, slightly mad look on Tim's face disturbed him, and he coughed, to play for time. He said "I presume my daughter has given her consent?"

Tim said "I've told her she must walk! I insist that she walks with me back down the aisle."

Mr. Pringle said "I'm the one who will be giving her away; I must take her up the aisle."

Tim said "You can wheel her up the aisle if you wish, Sir. But she'll walk back down the aisle with me!"

Mr. Pringle started to protest "The pain! – you can't be so cruel." But Tim interrupted him "My wife" he said "will walk!"

Mr. Pringle sat silent; worried, wondering. Wondering how this young man who'd been as soft as plasticine could have become as hard as an Iron Cross.

"Where will you live?" Mr. Pringle said "You could both live here. Helen will need my help, whenever you're out at work, or away." It was what Tim had wanted him to say; he had planned it.

Mr. Pringle rambled on "Helen will need financial help. You can't be expected to support a cripple."

Tim said "I take it then, that we have your blessing?" and Mr. Pringle said "Can I offer you a drink?"

Tim joined Helen in the garden, and Mr. Pringle followed with a tray, with glasses and sherry. He poured the sherry and said "Bless the bride!"

It was on the promenade at Blackpool that Helen felt the iron and the cross. But, even so, she was almost happy. She never could be really happy, not since that terrible day; she could never forget that she was a cripple in a wheelchair. It wasn't only the bitterness and the pain – it was the loss! She hated Gerald, but what she'd lost was love. But still, that afternoon at Blackpool, she was almost happy.

It was a glorious Blackpool afternoon, a once-in-a-summer afternoon, with all England happy and out for a spree. Even the slump was half forgotten, and a new King like a film star was on the throne: a King who'd been Prince Charming, and was now to be King for a year.

There was nothing to warn Helen that, this afternoon, she was going to feel the iron of the cross. She and Tim went for days-out so often; she'd come to expect it, especially since they'd been engaged. Anyway, she couldn't help telling herself, forgetting for a moment that she was the one who was crippled and had far more to lose than Tim; anyway, she thought, Tim did get a car out of it; the exclusive use of a car.

Blackpool was one of Helen's favourite places: it was an easy run from Liverpool, and there was plenty of life in Blackpool. It wasn't one of those empty places that she hated, like Wales.

Tim pulled up behind the line of cars parked along the prom. They were parked near to one of the piers, and there was steam-organ music from the Pier coming through the open windows of the car. There were trams going towards the Tower, and a little aeroplane pulling a banner through the sky, advertising Beecham's Pills.

They sat in the car, with the windows open: the tide was in, and there were waves. Helen said "Darling. Will you wheel me along the pier?"

She loved the pier: to be amongst all the people there and in the midst of life.

They paid their pennies and the attendant came to unlock the gate, for the wheelchair to bypass the turnstile. They stopped for a minute to watch the pierrots, then they went on, past the booths of the instant-portrait artists and the fortune-tellers, to the ballroom over the sea, where there was a tea-dance, and couples dancing the foxtrot like professionals, except that they were all frowning with concentration – unlike professionals, who would have been wearing a professional smile.

"Oh Tim!" Helen exclaimed "How I wish I could dance again!"

"Come on then" he said, and she laughed at the absurdity of it; but, when she looked-up at him,. she saw that he meant it. It was that look on his face, half-glazed and half-mad, that she was beginning to dread.

"Come on!" he said, and this time it was an order; an order from a Blackshirt officer disguised in plain clothes. He pushed the wheelchair, away from the dancers, and onto the deck of the pier where it was private, but they could still hear the music:

"No!" she cried out in panic "No, Tim!"

He was holding her, under her arm; she'd never thought of him as being strong: he'd been such a rabbit on the tennis court, compared with Gerald; but now he was strong as an Iron Cross. After all, he'd been a Blackshirt, now, for two years and he'd followed the training schedule and done the keep-fit exercises ordered by the leader. The Germans had their Führer, and had trained madly for him for the Olympics; the Italians had their Duce and had marched with him on Rome; and the

Blackshirts had their Leader, Oswald Mosley, and Tim would have followed Mosley to hell.

He was lifting Helen, under her arms, and her legs were dangling; useless. She had hold of him, clutching at him and digging her nails into his skin, through his shirt, in panic, like a woman drowning, or clinging to a cliff-edge, over an abyss. But he was strong; a Blackshirt officer. When she started to pant, and the pant became a scream, he shouted into her ear "Dance, damn you! Or I'll drop you."

She was struggling to overcome her panic, and to struggle free; and the pain was too terrible for her even to cry. But the pain was in her legs, that had been numb, ever since that terrible day. And that first, unexpected sensation in her legs made her want to scream with hope, through the pain.

Tim was moving to the music, and holding her up; taking all her weight. She was shapeless as a sack: during all those months in a wheelchair she'd lost her shape, and the shame of that hit her now. Only her arms were strong: her arms had the strength of the chairbound cripple who has to lift her bodyweight with her arms. Helen's arms were strong, and she was gripping Tim with all her strength. She'd lost the will to struggle against him, and she was crying "Oh, Tim! I'm so ashamed. I'm a helpless, ugly sack!"

"Move your legs!" he ordered.

It made her panic, and she said "My legs won't take any weight."

"I won't drop you" he said "Just move your legs in time to the music."

He was moving very slowly, in time to the music and panting with the effort of supporting her weight. However strong he'd become from Mosley's exercises, he was still not a big man, and Helen was just a sack.

But her legs were moving: swinging free above the floor; it was the first time she'd been able to move her legs since the terrible day. After a while Tim said "I'll have to put you down now, Helen. It's a strain."

He helped her into the wheelchair, but he folded-away its footrest, so her legs were unsupported and dangling free.

He said "Keep moving! Move your legs to the music."

It was painful, and tiring, and she wanted to rest, but he kept-on, ordering her not to stop. It was his willpower and not hers that made her go on.

At last the music stopped and it was like a reprieve from the rack. Tim said "You'll walk, Helen! – You'll walk, and we'll be married before the year's out."

It had started to blow, and waves were slapping the pier-supports; and there was spray on the wind. He pushed her to the end of the pier, and it was like being on a liner at sea.

Helen said "Sometimes I day-dream about being on a cruise."

"Why not?" Tim said, "Reach up and hold onto the rail. Pretend you're on a ship."

She did as he told her, and, with his help, and a struggle, she was free of the wheelchair and bent over the rail. Tim took the wheelchair away, and stood beside her, with his arm around her. Then he bent his head, and kissed her on the lips. It wasn't a tender kiss; it was the kiss of a Blackshirt officer taking control.

Helen said "I'm tired. It's a strain, holding myself up by my arms."

He said "Can you walk as far as the wheelchair?" He'd wheeled it about a yard away.

"No" she said "You know I can't."

"You will!" he said.

He had to prise her fingers from the rail, and she was sobbing "You're cruel Tim! You're cruel!"

She stumbled, and they nearly fell to the deck together, but he held her. "Walk!" he shouted "Walk, damn you!"

The cruel words shocked her, and, painfully, she began to move her legs. He was holding her up, but only partially, and she was moving – moving; pulled by a pain that was like the pain of the rack, towards the chair.

At last she slumped down into the chair, and she was weeping with the agony of it; too tired even to protest. She looked up at him, with a pitiful look; and, pitilessly he looked down.

"Every day!" he said "You will practice walking every day!"

He wheeled her back, through the people and the pierrots, and bought choc-ices from a man on a Wall's tricycle; and Helen had to stifle the memory of that golden carefree afternoon when Gerald had bought ices at Llandudno. Tim pushed the wheelchair beside a bench, so he could sit, and they sat in the sunshine eating their choc-ices and looking at the sea.

Tim said "Next time we come to Blackpool, Helen, you'll be walking, and we'll be married."

She said "Will we go out somewhere next weekend?"

"Next Sunday I'm on duty in London" he replied "There's an important rally in Victoria Park."

She tried not to show her disappointment. "You mustn't miss an important rally" she said.

Tim started to speak faster and louder, with the tell-tale glazed expression that frightened her. He was shouting "It's the damned Jews again! And the Reds! – We thought we'd smashed them two years ago, at Olympia."

It frightened Helen, all this shouting about Jews, in case people overheard and there was a scene.

"Hush" she said "You never know who's listening." She'd begun to dread the way he was always going on about Jews.

But he took no notice. He carried on, as if he was addressing a public meeting "Two years ago, Mosley was on top, at Olympia. We smashed the Reds at Olympia, Helen."

People were stopping to see what he was shouting about. "Please, Tim!" Helen said. She was thinking how some of the people that were stopping looked Jewish – there were always Jews at holiday places, running the booths and the funfair; making a quick quid or two.

Tim said "Mosley was betrayed! The newspapers – Lord Rothermere with his Daily Mail and his Evening News – . They used to support Mosley, but they've sold-out to the Jews! Jewish money has silenced the British Press, Helen. It's an International conspiracy of Jews, like Hitler says. The Blackshirts have got to fight back."

"Oh, Tim" Helen said "I'm frightened, Tim."

He kept-on "Where would Germany be now, if Hitler had been frightened of Jews and Reds?"

She said "Hitler's cruel, Tim. Even Jews deserve better than Hitler."

"Silence!" he ordered, and it was the Blackshirt officer who spoke "Remember Gerald Rinkman! – Rinkman was cruel, and you're the one in pain!"

She was silenced and he went on, but more quietly "The Jews of the East End are on the march. There will be five-thousand Blackshirts in Victoria Park next Sunday to Smash them."

But, next Sunday, it wasn't quite like that. True, there were five-thousand Blackshirts, and more, in Victoria Park, but there were also six-hundred policemen, many of them mounted.

Mosley made his big speech, and Tim felt the familiar electric thrill as the Leader's inspiration came to him across the crackle of the loudspeakers. They were still Fascists, the Leader announced; they were still his loyal Blackshirts. But the time had come to appeal to all British Patriots, of all Political Parties, and their title would be abbreviated simply to the

British Union.

Then the leader inspected his troops, and gave the Fascist salute as they marched past him. It brought tears to Tim's eyes, so intensely did he worship the man.

But the Jews and the Reds stayed away, and battle was not joined that day.

The East End of London had become a Jewish fortress, and as the Jews refused to come out of their fortress, Mosley made the big decision to take his challenge to the Jews. The call went out to every Blackshirt in Britain, and October the fourth was to be the day.

Helen had a premonition of danger – it hadn't seemed quite so ominous during the Summer, when Tim's trips to London had been like him going off to a summer camp; a bit like the boy-scouts. But now it was into Autumn, and storm-clouds were over Europe and threatening Britain. A few Blackshirts had already gone to fight for Franco's Fascists in Spain, where the reddest Reds from Britain had joined the other side. But Mosley said he needed all his men around him, and they shouldn't go to Spain until they'd won at home.

Tim was determined to join his Leader in London on October the fourth.

"Don't go" Helen pleaded.

But the glazed look came over Tim's face "Remember your own pain" he said "Your pain and my duty! I've got to face up to the Jews!"

The Blackshirt rallying-point was at the Royal Mint, near Tower Bridge; and there were more Blackshirts there than Tim had ever seen – not only from London, but from Leicester and Manchester and everywhere.

Tim felt so proud; there must have been fifteen-thousand at least: a black-shirted army as disciplined as Hitler's S.S.

They formed-up in four groups, under their officers,

and their Leader, Sir Oswald Mosley, addressed each group in turn. The threat was from the Reds and the Jews, he announced, but Blackshirt discipline would surely prevail.

They began to march, and it was a splendid thing to be part of that march; to be a Blackshirt officer like Tim, with high boots and a black cap. They'd left the Tower of London behind them now, and they were marching towards the enemy; right into the heart of the enemy fortress.

The police marched along with them: there were thousands of policemen; nearly as many policemen as Blackshirts. They came to Cable Street, and a lorry had been overturned across the street. There was a sound: a primitive, deafening roar of enmity and hate. It was the Reds and the Jews – Scum, as Mosley called them. "Scum!" Tim kept saying to himself as he marched "Vermin! – fit only for extermination."

The Police requested Mosley to halt, and the Blackshirt columns stopped: still, silent and disciplined; while the maddened enemy mob surged up to them and screamed.

The Blackshirt army stood motionless – silent and uniformed and disciplined – while the Red mob roared. The Red mob roared and surged, and, all around it, at its fringes, mobsters hurled cobblestones, and brickbats and oaths. Occasionally a mounted policeman charged and made an arrest, but the police knew that they were impotent to control the maddened mob: a mob of venom more virulent than a tarantula's.

"A mob! – A mere mob" Tim was saying to himself. He wasn't frightened, but he was moved by a hatred equal to the hatred shown by the mob. "Discipline" he was thinking "What has this maddened mob got, compared with our Discipline?"

He looked again, and the mob was even closer; and he saw just what it was that the mob had got: numbers! He saw their numbers, and, for the first time, he felt fear. The numbers of the maddened mob defied belief, unless you could see them as Tim was seeing them now in their tens of thousands; hundreds of thousands perhaps. The mob was pouring out of the East End in the way that a football crowd pours out of a stadium after the final whistle.

The Blackshirt columns stood to attention and stood their ground; Tim was proud of that. The mob screamed and surged around the upturned lorry, and the police made a baton-charge. The senior police officer begged Mosley not to advance. Mosley was a realist, and blood would have been on his head, if he'd refused. So, he gave the order to about-turn and he marched his men away. If Tim hadn't been a Blackshirt, he'd have cried.

That was the last time Tim wore his black shirt in public. The Jews had won, with the help of the Reds and he couldn't bear to think about it. Some of Tim's Blackshirt pals did go off to Spain to fight against the Reds, but Tim's heart wasn't in it any more. He put his uniform away in the wardrobe, and, anyway, quite soon afterwards, the Government passed the Public Order Act banning uniforms. So the uniform stayed in the wardrobe, hanging, with the high boots under it.

Sometimes Tim would open the wardrobe door, as if it was the door of a tabernacle, and gaze on the uniform; and, sometimes, he would put the uniform on and stand in front of the mirror, as if he was gazing at an icon. It was his secret, and it gave him the strength to face something he could never acknowledge: the victory of the Jews at Cable Street. Only much later did he share his secret, and even then, only with one person: with Helen, who was by then his wife.

She'd come upon him inadvertently, which was surprising, because, in her crippled state, she found it hard to move quietly. But he was so preoccupied, almost mesmerised, that he did not hear her when she came clumsily into the little room which Tim used as a dressing-room.

She stood at the door, holding onto the door-handle for support, and, after a while, he sensed her presence. He turned on her, fearing her mockery. But she said "Tim – you look so wonderful!"

His expression changed from anger to pleasure; he clicked the heels of his high boots, and he gave the Fascist salute.

"Come here!" he ordered; but she could not move quickly. He strode across, to hold her, and, grasping her hard, he led her to the bedroom and onto the bed.

He wasn't tender, but she wasn't looking for tenderness. He took her like a bully, pausing only to unbutton his black trousers. It was short, and the thrust of him sent pictures through her mind like a newsreel film accelerated by a projector gone mad. They were pictures of a thousand stamping jackboots, trampling over the face of a Jew, and the Jew was Gerald Rinkman.

When it was done she said "Oh Tim! – You're wonderful when you're in your uniform! – I can understand why women worship Hitler. Why they worship Mussolini!"

He stood-up, off her, and looked down at her; he felt like Siegfried; like Superman. He fastened his buttons and he straightened his tunic; then he gave the Fascist salute, turned smartly, and marched out of the room.

That was the first time, but not the last. Sometimes, when they were alone, Helen would look at Tim and he'd recognise that look of submission. "Oh Tim" she'd say "If only you'd wear your uniform."

On other occasions he'd appear in front of her, all dressed-up. He'd be standing there at the bedroom door, and he'd give orders, and she'd comply; after all, you don't argue with a Blackshirt officer. Helen would comply, and the pictures would be flickering through her mind. The pictures weren't always quite the same: they were influenced by what she'd seen at the cinema, on the newsreels. Sometimes there were Fascist divebombers in Spain, and the howl of their engines in her ears; with machine-guns chattering and the bullets hitting hard. Each time there were different pictures, but always there were marching men in jackboots, trampling across the familiar face of a Jew.

But all this happened only after they were married. Before they married they were both – Helen and Tim – models of propriety.

The wedding was at the church on Mossley Hill. Tim's pals were there; the ones who'd stood up for him against Gerald at the Club, and who'd later joined the Blackshirts, and who now, like Tim, had to hide their black shirts away. One of the Blackshirts was Best Man, though he wasn't that close a friend to Tim; not really close, like Gerald had been. The idea that Gerald might have been Best Man made Tim want to spit. He refused to let himself think about Gerald.

Tim and the Best Man were at the front of the church, with the wedding-guests behind them, including Tim's other Blackshirt pals, and the few girlfriends who'd stayed loyal to Helen. She'd had so many girlfriends, but many of them had proved false – either because they couldn't be bothered with a cripple, or because they couldn't stand Tim. There was only one bridesmaid, Helen's best friend who worshipped her, even now, even though she was a cripple: Pat Curry, the girl who was always behind the teacups at the Club.

The organ started-up, and everyone stood-up for the bride. There was a delay while the chauffeur of the bridal-car helped the bride's father with the wheelchair, and then everyone was turning around to look at Helen in the wheelchair, all flushed and pretty in white satin, with Mr. Pringle in his morning-coat pushing her up the aisle.

Just like Tim, Helen refused to let herself think of

Gerald, but all the long way up the aisle she was thinking of him. Well, it wasn't really a long way, but Mr. Pringle was slow.

So, all the long, slow journey up the aisle, with everybody staring at her, Helen wasn't seeing them at all; she was remembering a black-pearl of a night by Lake Windermere, and her passion for a handsome, heartless Jew. Tears welled, and she cursed her crippled body; then she looked up and she was close to Tim Leston in his morning-coat, and the Parson in his surplice was asking her to make her marriage vows.

The service was short, and swift, and then it was time for Helen to face her ordeal. She looked up at Tim, in the hope that the words of the service might have touched his heart; that he would smile down at his bride whom he'd vowed to cherish, and wheel her away – or even carry her off in his arms, with all the strength of a Blackshirt. But what she saw was not the smiling face of a bridegroom, but the pitiless stare of a Fascist officer.

"Now!" he ordered, and she found herself rising-up to the order, like one who's hypnotised. Oh! the pain of it! The shock and the pain – and her determined, hideous smile, trying to conceal her pain from the world.

There were voices of surprise from the guests; and then, clutching the arm that Tim held out to her, and forcing herself not to cry-out, Helen turned and began slowly to shuffle down the aisle. The best man followed, with the bridesmaid, pushing the empty chair, and, behind them, the guests inched forward at the painful pace of the bride.

At the church door, Helen stopped, panting with the pain and effort. She said "My wheelchair – please Tim!" but he ignored her. He said "Smile for the photographer! – Stand straight!"

She was nearly crying with the pain, and Tim said "Our

wedding-photo will be in the evening paper – let's show the Jew!"

Helen let-go of the church wall, and, clinging only to her husband's arm, she forced herself to smile at the camera.

Tim moved-in with Helen and her father, as had been arranged. The old man was pathetically glad to have Tim to help him with Helen, and it was almost as if Tim and Helen now owned the house with her father there as a lodger. The old man was failing fast; it was as if he'd used-up all his reserves of strength in looking after Helen, and now, at last, he could give-in to old age. He took to coming downstairs later and later in the mornings, until his role and that of his daughter – the role of nurse and patient – were reversed. Tim was out at work all day, and Helen had to force herself to move about the house: to search in cupboards, and to make tea. She managed, by clinging onto furniture, and, when there was no furniture to cling to, she improvised. Sometimes she even crawled across the floor. Then, one day, she found she was walking: painfully limping, it's true, but, nonetheless walking without support. At first she didn't realise; and then, when she realised, she flopped into a chair and cried.

That evening, when she heard Tim outside on the drive, Helen was at the door to greet him. "At last!" he cried "It's willpower! – Willpower is omnipotent!"

"Your willpower, Tim," she said "Not mine."

He didn't argue, and, instead, he said "Hitler has marched into Austria. That's willpower!"

She caught her breath "Will it be war?"

"War?" he replied "No. Nobody but Hitler has got the willpower for war."

"I'm glad" she said. But he was shouting "The Jews will soon know about war!"

It frightened her, that look on his face: half mad, half cruel. She leant-back against the wall – she was still not strong

– and whispered "Oh, Tim! – Let's leave the Jews alone! Look: I can walk again now. Let's forget Gerald Rinkman and the Jews."

He was angry and he shouted "Never! – I'll never forget the way he treated you."

But he was remembering, not so much Helen's pain, as his own: his pain when his girl had been stolen from him by a Jew, and when he did get her back it was only because she was broken and unwanted, and ditched by the Jew.

That night Mr. Pringle died. He went out smiling, in his armchair.

After the funeral, Tim and Helen talked. Helen had got over her tears, and she said "He was the best father, Tim. I'll always miss him."

Tim said "We'll both miss him, Helen. But, he was smiling when he died; he lived to see his daughter walk again."

She said "He'd you to thank for that, Tim. You were the answer to his worst fears over what would become of me when he died."

He said "Your father had one great disappointment – that he never had a grandchild."

Helen's eyes filled with tears. "I'm sorry, Tim" she whispered. Oh, she'd tried so hard – it wasn't that she was incapable of making love. At first it had been painful, nearly as painful as trying to walk. She'd forced herself to make love in the same way she'd forced herself to walk. Or, rather, in both activities – in walking and in lovemaking – Tim had given the orders, and Helen had obeyed.

Lovemaking, she was thinking – love could mean so many different things: a forbidden memory of heaven beside a lake; or submission to jackboots and a black uniform.

She said "I'm sorry, Tim. But we've time yet, to have a child." She said it, but she didn't really believe it. Her instinct told her that, when she'd been crippled and half-paralysed, her ability to have children had been left behind, there, in the ditch.

Tim said "There's something I have to say, Helen. Your father has left you a rich woman. Your husband's business should reflect that."

Helen said "The Stocks and Shares that daddy left me will provide a good income. We don't need to take risks."

Tim made an effort not to show his impatience. He said "It isn't only a question of income; it's prestige. The other professions – Accountants and Lawyers – they condescend towards Surveyors like me." He saw that the idea of that upset her, and he pressed his advantage "The worst people for condescension are the Jews. Especially Gerald Rinkman, with his swanky office and his swanky cars."

Helen raised her voice "You know I never want to hear that name! – If Gerald Rinkman condescends, then you must have an office to be proud of, Tim. And we'll change the car for one as good as his."

Tim was staring, with that look of his that frightened her. He was saying "If only our great leader, Sir Oswald Mosley, was Prime Minister! – If only people would recognise what Hitler has done for Germany!"

Helen found herself unable to meet his half-mad stare "There's terrible news coming out of Germany" she said.

But Tim wasn't listening. He was shouting "I don't believe half of it! – If a few more people had followed Mosley we'd not be in the mess we're in today."

Helen said "The Blackshirts were beaten by the London Jews. Driven-out by a rabble of East End tailors."

"Traitor!" he shouted, with his hand raised. It seemed as if he was about to strike her. "We were betrayed!" he screamed "I was there, remember? I saw it. It wasn't just the Jews – we'd have beaten the Jews. But a hundred-thousand Reds were with the Jews. Mosley didn't want bloodshed, so he marched us away."

The truth of it still rankled, even after two years. Oh, there were plenty of good excuses! – the impossible odds of ten-to-one against the Blackshirts. But still, it was a defeat that Tim couldn't face. He said "When we're needed we'll be ready, Helen. That's why I keep my uniform. Ready for Mosley's call."

Helen said "What if there's a war, Tim? What if England goes to war with Germany? – They hang traitors, Tim."

Her words gave him pause; then, at last, he said "I'll never fight for the Jews." He paused again, and added quietly, "You're a cripple, Helen. You can't manage without me. I'll get exemption from military service on compassionate grounds."

Helen said "I hope so, Tim. This war in Spain is terrible."

"Terrible but necessary" he said "Franco will smash the Reds. You'll see."

Tim got his prestigious office, and they bought a prestigious car; a car to make heads turn, a Humber limousine. When they saw Tim's new car, or visited Tim's new office, the professional men, the lawyers and accountants stopped condescending. But they didn't send him clients, at least not enough clients to sustain the car, and the office, and the secretary who sat in the office as receptionist and did the typing.

It wasn't long before Tim had to ask Helen for more money. This time it frightened her. She said "What if we spend all daddy's money, Tim?"

Tim interrupted her "It takes time to establish a prestigious business" he said.

Helen said "Do you really need a secretary, Tim? – Couldn't you wait until you're established enough to pay her from the business?"

He turned on her "I'd be a laughing-stock, Helen –

losing my secretary so soon! Starting out big, and ending small! Do you want them all sniggering at me, Helen? Do you want to see Gerald Rinkman laughing at your husband?"

She had nothing to say, so he pressed his point. "Do you realise how much you depend on me, Helen?" he asked "I drive you everywhere. I wait for you, and help you back into the car. I do all your messages, and all the shopping. I can't devote as much time as I'd like to my business, Helen."

She knew it was true, and, after a pause, she whispered "Don't think I'm not grateful, Tim. How much more money will you need?"

The war came, and everyone was being called-up. Tim got his exemption – it was true that Helen could not have managed without him, and there was nobody else to look after her.

Nothing much changed for Tim and Helen. There was the blackout, of course, and, after a time, petrol was rationed. But Tim had a priority allocation of petrol coupons for his business, and because of his wife's disability.

Tim's business thrived. Many surveyors had been called up, and most of those who hadn't were too old, or too physically unfit to do the inaccessible surveys. Tim built himself a reputation as a man for the difficult jobs: going up ladders into lofts, or onto rooves. And he was meticulous about his written reports: they might have seemed pompous, but they were detailed and accurate. Professional men, lawyers in particular, began to give him their grudging respect, and, what's more, they regularly employed him to draw-up plans for them, and, sometimes, as an expert witness on property matters in court.

The bombs came. The nights were terrifying, and Tim had no choice but to make a contribution towards the war effort. He took his turn at firewatching, up on the church tower, with a pair of binoculars and a tin hat; while the bombers droned overhead towards the docks, with the thump! thump! of the bombs, and ships and warehouses all ablaze against the black sky.

After one night of firewatching, Tim got home tired-out, and all grimy from the smoke and the damp night air. He threw down his tin-hat, and the gas-mask he had to carry, but had never, yet, had to wear; the ugly thing that, somehow, seemed to symbolise the war.

Helen said "Hitler's no longer a hero, even for you, Tim."

"My heart's still not in the war" he said "They've banned the British Union and they've interned Mosley – Mosley, who's the greatest patriot in Britain!" He bent to unlace his boots "If only they'd listened to Mosley" he said bitterly "We wouldn't be having this damned blitz."

Nobody knew quite how much Tim owed to the war. As more and more young surveyors went into the forces, he could pick his jobs and name his fees. Not many people were moving house, it's true, but there was the business of claims against the War Damage Commission, and plenty of building repairs. Tim was good at drawings and plans, and the hazards from damaged property brought him opportunities as an expert witness in Court. Someone might be injured and looking for compensation: if they'd hit their head on a threshold, or tripped over an uneven pavement, Tim was usually the man the lawyers engaged to measure-up and to write a report. Taken all-in-all, the war was a good time for Tim.

CHAPTER EIGHT

After the war, for a time, Tim continued to prosper. Servicemen were being demobbed, and looking for houses to live in, and so were all the bombed-out people. Tim even got some work from the Government's council-house building programme.

Then, for no apparent reason, Tim's business fell away.

One morning he was lingering over breakfast; he was sitting, with the morning paper propped against the teapot, and nervously nibbling his toast. Helen was watching him: he never went out early any more, in the busy way he used to rush out of the house. He had that intense, half-mad look that she dreaded.

His pent-up feelings burst. "Jews!" he shouted "There's always trouble from Jews!"

"Hush!" she said, frightened in case someone might hear him shouting so loudly. It wouldn't do, to be heard shouting against Jews; not with the terrible photographs of the Nazi death-camps that had been in all the papers. She said "Oh Tim – how could you? The shame and the horror, Tim! Even you must feel pity for the Jews!"

But Tim wasn't listening. He was shouting "The Jews are too clever! – the way they've played on everybody's sympathy: the concentration camps; the death camps. – Now everybody's falling over themselves to help the Jews."

Helen was getting agitated "Don't shout, dear, please."

Tim sneered "The bitterness and the pain, Helen! Have you forgotten Gerald Rinkman?"

Helen replied in a low voice, as if it pained her to speak "Never mention Gerald Rinkman. I thought we'd put Gerald Rinkman out of our lives for ever."

Tim said "As long as Gerald Rinkman was away at the war, we could forget him. But now he's back in Liverpool! – Colonel Rinkman, M.C.! How do you like that, Helen? – A war hero with a Military Cross. What's more, he's standing for Liverpool City Council."

He thrust the newspaper at her, and it had a photograph of a handsome Jew in uniform with medal-ribbons on his chest, and the crown and stars of a Colonel on his epaulettes.

Helen stared in shock at the photograph, and all the old feelings of attraction came over her, mixed-up with hate.

Tim went on bitterly "They're all coming home, Helen; all the professional men are coming back." He paused, in an effort to compose himself "Why do you think I'm no longer out early in the mornings? Have you thought about that Helen?"

Helen didn't reply, and Tim said "During the war, they were all glad to employ me, Helen. But now it's Major this and Colonel the other. They're keeping all the business amongst themselves, Helen – the officers and the Jews!"

"You're being silly, Tim!" she exclaimed "Officers, perhaps – but not Jews!"

"Don't dare say I'm silly!" he shouted "Jews have got a stranglehold on this City! With Jews like Gerald Rinkman on the Council, what hope is there for my business?"

"You're a good surveyor" Helen said "Surely that counts?"

Tim said "If Rinkman and his Jewish friends are going to look big, I'll have to look even bigger. The office has run down during the war. I'll need a bigger office, Helen. A more impressive office."

"Oh, Tim!" She was almost crying "That's what nearly bankrupted us before the war; all that extravagance. It was only the war that saved us, Tim."

But he wasn't listening. He was saying "Do you want to give Gerald Rinkman something to sneer about, Helen? – I'll show Gerald Rinkman! I'll show the Jews!"

Helen said "There's not much of daddy's money left, Tim. What if we lose it all?"

Tim interrupted "You've admitted I'm a good Surveyor. I'm well respected; well-known." He paused, and looked hard at her, in that intense, mad way "You could do your part to bring-in more business, Helen. Through your friends. If any of your friends ever needs a surveyor, Helen, she should come to me."

So, Tim moved to a splendid new office in North John Street, above a fashionable men's outfitters. And he employed a smartly-dressed secretary to sit at a desk next to the window, where she could be seen by everyone in all the offices along the street, and especially from the Rinkman office.

But the response to the move was disappointing. Too few professional men-about-town chose to make their way upstairs from the men's outfitters to Tim's secretary, with a view to employing Tim in his professional capacity as a surveyor.

Tim lost money, but he was not prepared to lose face; not when Rinkman and Son, Solicitors and Commissioners for Oaths had their long-established office at the corner. So Tim started to look out for other ways of raising money.

The most obvious way was to profit from the sales of land as building sites. He had already been involved with several such projects on behalf of clients; in submitting plans and planning applications. Up to now, all Tim had got out of it was his fees, and he'd had no share in the hefty profit out of land when it was given the Midas-touch of Planning Consent for Development. He took another look at the garden: he'd have liked to think of it as his own garden, but Helen's father had made that almost impossible by the terms of his Will.

It wasn't a big garden; just a very pretty garden, the way it fell-away from the house, with the park and the trees beyond. It really would have spoiled the house to build in the garden, and it would have broken Helen's heart.

Nevertheless, Tim studied the Deeds of the house. He

hadn't much else to do, and it looked as if he was busy at his office desk, with a set of house Deeds in front of him.

The groundplan was simple and clear: the garden, and, beyond the garden-wall, the land which belonged to the City: parkland.

But... but... Tim looked again, why had he never noticed? – Probably because the garden wall obscured the view of the land immediately behind it. Of course! – the park must have been part of the Estate of some great house, long since demolished; but the strip of land immediately behind the garden wall, was not, strictly, in the park at all. Beyond the garden wall was another older wall; much older than Helen's house.

Tim searched the Deeds, snatching at one document after another. Ah! – here it was; just what he had suspected: the park itself was inviolable, but the strip of land was protected only by Restrictive Covenants. If only he could get hold of the strip of land cheaply from the City Council, and then challenge the Covenants successfully in the courts! He knew that, after a century or more, Restrictive Covenants were not necessarily binding. But he'd have to act carefully. First, he'd make an offer to the council, to buy the land without planning consent, and therefore cheap, on the pretext of extending Helen's garden. Then, he'd challenge the Covenants, get planning consent, and put up some speculative housing. He wouldn't employ an architect; he'd draw-up the plans himself. He'd show everybody what he could do! He wouldn't even need to employ a lawyer except for the conveyancing; – he'd show everyone what a good lawyer he might have been, if he hadn't been betrayed by a Judas; by a Jew. An architect and a lawyer too? Oh, yes! He'd show them! He smiled a smile of triumph: an architect, and a lawyer, and a master-builder, all at once! He'd employ sub-contractors, but he'd be the master. He'd supervise the building works himself. And the houses, when they were complete, and sold for a profit, would be an everlasting monument to Tim Leston the master-builder, famous throughout the world, like Wren or Vanburgh.

The secretary was out of the office and Tim was alone. On impulse he stood-up at his desk, and clicked his heels, and gave the Fascist salute.

But Tim didn't have long to enjoy his dream of glory.

The next morning was again a lovely summer's morning and Tim was enjoying his breakfast and looking out at the garden and the trees beyond; and thinking about the land between the garden, and the trees. He said "How I enjoy the breakfasts you cook for me, Helen! – To think of the years when you were so helpless!"

Helen smiled with pleasure, and sipped her tea. She said "It's easy to make a good breakfast when you can buy bacon and fresh eggs; not like during the war."

Tim picked-up the newspaper – he took the Liverpool Daily Post to keep up with the local news; he found the local property news indispensable for his work. He leant away from the table to make room to spread the newspaper, and – there it was! Another photograph of the man he hated: Liverpool City Councillor Gerald Rinkman; no longer in uniform, but in a smart city suit. Far too often Tim was having to endure Councillor Gerald Rinkman's photograph in the newspapers, and his confident, supercilious smile.

Tim started to read, and what he read blurred the print before his eyes and made his temples throb. He made a sound like an animal strangled in a snare.

"Tim!" Helen exclaimed in alarm.

"Read that!" he replied, choking out the words. And he thrust the newspaper at her.

She saw at once the hated, handsome face; and she read the words so quickly she could hardly comprehend them. She said "I don't understand."

Into that morning of sunshine and birdsong Tim's voice cut like a blizzard "The devil wants to destroy us both – to destroy you a second time, Helen."

Helen's reply was something between a whisper and a panic cry "Not again, Tim?"

Tim banged the table, so that the plates rattled, and a knife fell onto the floor "He's scheming to put-up buildings behind this house – behind your house, Helen."

The worst thing for Tim wasn't the proposed building; but that Rinkman, once more, had gained the upper hand. Rinkman had once stolen Tim's girl and now, he'd stolen Tim's plan.

Helen was saying "He can't do that Tim. Surely? The land beyond our garden is a public park."

Tim ignored her "Do you know what he's trying to build Helen? Did you read it? – A Jews' home! A home for Jewish refugees! – Behind this house, of all places, Helen! He wants to provoke me, Helen. He wants his revenge, like Shylock. He knows I'll never rest if we're overlooked by Jews."

Helen said weakly "You haven't explained, Tim. It's a public park."

"You don't know the half of it" – he was impatient with her and the way she was ignorant of her own house Deeds; forgetting that he, with all his professional experience, had studied them too late. "There's scrubland behind our garden wall; between our wall, and the old park wall. The City Council planned a road there years ago, but the road was never built. And now Councillor Gerald Rinkman has bought the land from the Council for the Jews."

All the bitterness was coming back, and Helen said "Surely he can't give me so much pain again?"

Tim said "Just look at that!" and he thrust a finger onto the newspaper "The council has already sold the land to the Jewish Refugees' Society." Bitterness and sarcasm filled his voice "What's more, the Planning Committee of the City Council has already approved plans. Who do you think is Chairman of the Planning Committee, Helen? – Councillor Gerald Rinkman! And which firm of solicitors is acting for the Jewish Refugees? – Rinkman and Son, of course!"

Helen stared at him dumbly through the tears, as Tim was thumping the table and shouting "And who do you think is Chairman of the Jewish Refugee Society? Who?" He stopped, unable to continue.

"Gerald Rinkman" she whispered "The Devil, Rinkman.. Beelzebub."

Tim sprang-up from his chair, with his eggs and bacon untouched on the plate "The Devil?" he shouted "You're right! – But the devil's in for a surprise. He's in for a fight!"

"Oh, Tim, No!" she said

"There are Restrictive Covenants on that land" he said "The courts will prevent him building." He was too bitter even to recognise the irony of it: the way that the Covenants, which had so lately been an irritating obstruction to his own plans for profit, had now become a bastion of hope.

Helen said "Be careful, Tim!"

But he was full of himself, and taking no notice. "Gerald Rinkman will have me to face: me, a Fellow of the Royal Institute of Chartered Surveyors, who could have been a lawyer too." He was shouting now, like Hitler on his podium at Nuremberg "I'll stand up to him! I'll never give-in to a Jew!"

At last, when he paused for breath, Helen said "What's a Restrictive Covenant, Tim?"

"A Restriction on the use of land" he said "All the land around here – the park; this plot your house is built on; and the strip of land in between – they were all part of one big Estate. The strip of land was sold, subject to a Covenant, restricting building-development."

"I'm so relieved" Helen said, but he cut her short. He

said "Sometimes Restrictive Covenants are overlooked and ignored; after a lapse of time, or a change of ownership. They have to be established in Court."

"I pray we never have to go to Court" she said.

"Sometimes the Court does over-rule a Covenant" he said "Or it refuses to enforce one. And often when somebody ignores a Covenant, or acts in defiance of a Covenant, he gets away with it. That's what Rinkman's hoping – he thinks he'll frighten us."

The idea that he'd lost his own chance of profit to the Jew was too galling for Tim to bear. Now his task was to establish the very same covenants he'd planned to overturn.

Helen said "How can he hope to have the Covenants declared void?"

"Money!" Tim said "The City Council always needs more money, and the sale of land with the benefit of planning consent is an easy way of raising money. Jews always have money; they fight with money."

"We'll have to move away" she was crying now "I never thought I'd have to leave this house. I love this house, Tim."

"We'll fight the Jew!" he said "I couldn't bear to give-in to the Jew."

She was still crying "Costs and lawyers' fees! The costs will break us, Tim. And we've already spent most of daddy's money."

"But, Helen" he said "Think of the bitterness and the pain! To give-in and run away; or, even worse, to endure a Jewish Home looming over us. Always there. Always."

"I still can't understand why he wants to do this to us. He won't get anything out of it for himself. The City Council will get all the money."

"His Jewish friends will get a splendid home" Tim replied bitterly "And the City Council will make a splendid profit – Councillor Rinkman gets the kudos both ways: amongst the Jews he becomes a sort of king; and, in a year or two, the Council elects him Mayor." He paused, in an effort to calm his seething soul "But his greatest satisfaction is a secret satisfaction: he gets his pound of flesh. He hates us Helen."

It was true, and not even Tim could guess at the intensity of Gerald Rinkman's loathing for all things Fascist. For Colonel Rinkman had been one of the first Allied Officers into the death camps; he'd come face to face with the unspeakable, and the unspeakable would haunt his nights for the rest of his life.

Helen was sobbing "The legal costs will be the death of us, Tim – as surely as a pound of flesh cut from our heart."

"You worry too much" Tim tried to reassure her "The costs won't be excessive. These cases are not at all like a full High-Court hearing."

She said "I hope you know what you're doing, Tim." – She so wanted to trust him and to look up to him. She wanted to believe that, between Gerald Rinkman and Tim Leston, Tim was the more able man; Tim, the Blackshirt officer. But secretly, she knew very well that Tim's black shirt and officer's cap had covered over a strange blend of rashness and ineptitude. The Blackshirt officer was really no match for the Jewish colonel with the Military Cross.

But Tim couldn't overlook the chance to show-off in his usual, over-confident way: the way Helen had come to mistrust, despite her longing for a husband who was masterful.

"Under Section 84 of the Law of Property Act, 1925" he was saying "A Statutory Chairman, a Judge, is appointed by the Lord Chancellor – by the Chancery Division of the High Court – to try the Case."

"Oh, Tim" Helen said "You seem to know all about everything."

"You're forgetting, my dear" he replied, with a

condescending smile "I might have been a great Lawyer, but for the Jew."

CHAPTER NINE

Helen spent the day of the court-hearing waiting for a telephone call. She knew that, if Tim won, he'd phone right away. But no call came, and, when she heard the car on the drive, she went to meet him with a heavy heart.

But it was still a shock to her when she saw him. He was shaking out of control, and the mad look she always dreaded was even more terrifying as it was mixed with tears.

"That damned Judge!" Tim choked "That damned Jew!"

He stumbled across the threshold, and Helen closed the door behind him. She tried to support him, but she hadn't the strength: she would always be a cripple, and she felt that most poignantly now, when she needed the strength that the Jew had stolen from her.

Tim fell into a chair. "The Judge set aside the Covenants" he croaked "It was because of Rinkman with his forked-tongue. The Judge ruled the Covenants to be unenforceable!"

He was coughing now, and inarticulate.

"I'll get you a drink" she said. But he gesticulated to stop her, and managed to blurt-out "I won't give-in Helen! – I'll expose him! – Using his privileged position on the City Council like that. It's completely unethical, Helen. What can you expect of a Jew?"

She was really frightened: his mad look had become frenzy. His eyes were staring - red and there were flecks of saliva on his lips. She said "Tim, Tim. Please be careful."

He sat up suddenly; bolt upright in the chair. "There will be a Jews' home overlooking us day and night. Jews staring at us over our own wall. Gerald Rinkman himself may even be there sometimes, looking down on us! Don't you care, Helen?"

"Of course I care." She was weeping "I care so deeply; so deeply – but, don't fight him, Tim. We've lost, but we've still got something left. He'll take everything, Tim. He'll destroy you; he'll destroy us both."

She was crawling now, on her knees; kneeling to him, with her hands clasped on his hands "Don't give him the chance to destroy us, Tim. Don't play into his hands."

Tim shouted out "The Jewish Community is certain to reward their Jewish City Councillor. That's bribery! – I'll expose it, Helen."

"Tim, Tim" she said "You need proof!"

"I'll put the newspapers onto it" he was shouting wildly "The newspapers will find proof."

They didn't sleep that night, and they hardly slept on subsequent nights, until the building work was started.

It was shocking how very soon the building work did start. Helen had imagined it would be months or even years. But it was only weeks. It happened on a lovely morning, early, before Tim had left for the office, and, when Helen heard the sound of it, she was sick – not just sick at heart, but really, physically sick, as if she had been caught by a sudden storm at sea.

The sounds were like a storm and as sudden: a sudden pneumatic drill that split the heavens and stunned the birds to silence, so that, when the drill paused for a minute, the heavens were as empty of music as the pit of hell. A concrete mixer began to grind and slosh, and, above it all, a workman was shouting to make himself heard by his mates.

It got worse every day, as the building rose higher, and, each morning at the breakfast table, Tim sat trembling; trying to ignore it, but, in reality, mesmerised and caught-up in a fascination of hate. Now it was Tim who was on the retreat, just as the Nazi Blackshirts, the Waffen S.S., had been forced to retreat in the end, in the face of tanks that had ground forward against them, as inexorable as concrete mixers.

When he could stand it no longer, Tim screamed "There's no peace, Helen! – That building; looming over us! – The noise; all day, every day; even on Sunday! – How the Jews hate our Sundays, and want to spoil them. Those drills! – They're drilling into us Helen! Oh, the bitterness and the pain!"

Now it was Helen who showed herself to be the strong one, with the strength of steel that's tempered, and twisted by pain. She said "I'll never let Gerald Rinkman drive me out of my house; out of daddy's house. I'll never give-in, I'd rather die!"

Tim looked at her and he knew her words weren't the usual trite cliché. He knew she'd die before she'd give-in. He said "I wrote to the newspapers about Rinkman. They won't publish. – You know why? – Because the Jews control the newspapers, that's why! They control the newspapers like they control everything else. But the newspapers aren't the only power in the land – Mosley stood up to the Jews, Helen! Mosley's still alive; he'll not let us down."

She said "How I admired you in your black shirt and your high boots, Tim! I could never admire a man who gave-in to the Jews."

In a strange way it was Helen, now, who'd become the strong one. He said "You were always so nervous about it, Helen. About standing-up against Jews."

She said "We can't afford to be nervous any longer, if we want to stop these Jews."

He said "I'll start with those building workers. I'll make them listen to me."

There were four men, up on the scaffolding, with bricks and buckets of mortar. Tim opened the french-window and went outside – they rarely opened any windows now, because of the noise – and the noise hit him like a fist. He shouted "You there! Can you hear me?" His shout was loud, and carried the authority of a Blackshirt officer; and the men must have heard him, for, one by one the noises died away: the concrete mixer's grind faded; then the whine of the electric drill; and, finally, the ribald banter of the men.

Tim shouted again "Do you know who you're working for? – You're working for Jews; the international conspiracy of Jews."

The men were slow to react, and then they started laughing. "Listen to 'im" one of them shouted, in a broad scouse accent. "'E's a nutter!" And another called out "If you're bothered about Ikey Moses, wack – Ikey's my best mate."

They all laughed at that; it wasn't even jeering laughter. They weren't taking Tim seriously enough to jeer.

The building noises started-up again, and Tim was left looking foolish. Those ignorant oafs had made a fool of him. It was unbearable. "Reds!" he shouted "You're all Reds" and he thrust his arm in the Fascist salute. How he longed for a posse of Blackshirts like the ones who'd beaten the Reds insensible at Olympia in nineteen-thirty-four!

He went indoors and shut the french window behind him; shutting out some of the noise. Helen said "We can't even enjoy our own garden. All we can do is hide indoors."

Tim said "Before the war, lots of important people supported Mosley – even the Prince of Wales, who's Duke of Windsor now. I'll write to them all. They'll back me up."

"You must have proof, Tim" she said, and he replied "Rinkman the City Councillor and Rinkman the Jewish Lawyer: the same man acting for both parties! – It stinks, Helen. Stinks of corruption! – What more proof do I need? I'll write to the President of the Law Society; to the Lord Lieutenant of Lancashire; the Lord Chancellor... I'll do it now, today!"

It had to be today; Tim had to do something to smash the jeering scouser-Red whose best mate was Ikey Mo'.

Helen could hardly fail to notice the expression on Tim's face: the half-mad look and the staring eyes. But this time her anxiety was tempered by her own obsession with revenge. She followed Tim to the front door, and, as he drove away, the sound of the exhaust reminded her of what exhaust-sounds always reminded her; of a car with a roar like a lioness; and of her own poor body that had been so badly mauled.

Tim drove straight to his office and began himself to type, for what he was typing had to be secret, even from his own secretary. He typed deliberately and obsessively, pausing only to form a phrase powerful enough to indict Rinkman; he typed with his lips fixed in a mirthless smile.

He demanded redress. The surveyor and the frustrated lawyer that was Tim Leston demanded substantial damages for loss of value and amenity; and for distress. As a surveyor he put a value on Helen's home, both as it had been, and as it was now, under an alien shadow. He pointed out that Rinkman and Son were solicitors to the Jewish Refugees' Association, and that Rinkman himself was a Jew. He pointed out that Rinkman was also a City Councillor, and had used his influence to get planning consent for a Jewish Refugees' Home. That, in the Chancery Division of the High Court, the learned Judge sitting as Statutory Chairman had set-aside Restrictive Covenants. And that Gerald Rinkman, Solicitor and City Councillor, had masterminded the whole operation for personal profit and out of personal malice.

He made duplicates of the letter, and signed each copy. Then he folded the letters into envelopes and addressed them: one to the Lord Mayor of Liverpool; one to the Lord Chancellor; and one to the President of the Law Society.

Two replies came by return of post. They came not to the office, but to the house, as Tim had requested. It was already a morning of nerves cut-raw by the scream of a mechanical saw. First, Tim opened the reply from the President of the Law Society, and his face twisted as he read it "We'll have to fight-on alone Helen" he choked "No help from the President of the Law Society!" He opened the second reply, the one from the Lord Chancellor, and read-out the few curt lines. "They're all the same" he said "They may not themselves be Jews, but all lawyers are like a mafia in the pay of Jews."

Helen was looking into her teacup, too upset to trust herself to speak. The mechanical saw screamed to a crescendo, and it made her want to scream too. She said "We can't fight them, Tim. We can't fight the whole world on our own."

He said "We've no choice but to fight, Helen. If people like ourselves don't fight, the world will be taken-over by the Jews."

"Jews! Jews! Jews!" she was screaming now just like the saw "You'll destroy us both, Tim, with your obsession against Jews."

He said "Remember Rinkman, remember the bitterness and the pain."

She said "I never forget it, Tim – how could I forget, when I'll always limp? But we must try to forget. The more we fight, the more we suffer. We are the ones who'll suffer; not the Jews."

Tim said "I'll never give-in. I'd rather lose everything than give-in."

"Oh, Tim!" she cried "I've hardly a friend left now: only Pat Curry. And soon I'll have no money – perhaps not even a house – because of your vendetta against Jews."

He paused, stunned cold by her words "Even you, Helen?" he said "Are even you against me?"

She said "I had a few friends – good friends who stood by me even when I was crippled. They can accept that. But they can't accept my husband – you never stop, Tim. Did you know that? Wherever we happen to be; whatever it is we're talking about – you always bring up the Jews. Then you start to hold-forth. Ranting, I've heard people call it. You've got a captive audience, and they sit there, feeling bored or embarrassed, and unable to get in a word in the face of your ranting."

She was crying now. She'd never believed she'd be able to bring herself to say what she'd just said. The tears were running unchecked and she went on, through the tears "I've lost most of my friends, Tim, nobody ever visits."

He said, cruelly "You call them friends?"

She was caught up in emotion and unable to stop; everything came pouring out, now that the cork was pulled. She was pouring it all out, and he couldn't stop her. "That's not the only thing" she was saying "You take advantage, Tim. You try to take advantage of people's friendship, to make money."

"No!" he shouted "Only Jews do that!"

"That's what they're all saying" she said "They say you must be a Jew yourself the way you behave. That you rant against Jews to cover your own Jewishness – I haven't forgotten about that grandmother of yours, Tim."

"Quiet!" he shouted. But even the shouted order of a Blackshirt officer was not enough to silence her.

"When you're not ranting against Jews" she went on "You deliberately try to get my friends to talk about houses: about their own houses; or you make suggestions about houses they might like to buy. What you're really trying to do is to put them under an obligation."

"Everyone's interested in houses" Tim said defensively.

Distracted as she was, she still made an attempt to mimic one of her friends – to try to make him see; somehow, to make him understand "I had such an interesting talk with Tim" she gushed, and it was painful the way she forced herself to act it out "Tim told me all about dry rot and how to treat it. I've been worried about dry rot for years."

"Nobody's more of an expert on dry rot than I am." Tim

said.

"My friends think it's just been friendly conversation. But then they get a bill in the post. You send-out bills for professional advice, Tim."

"My professional advice is worth money" he snapped.

"But my friends never thought they were employing you" she protested "And now I've hardly any friends left. They're all frightened they'll be the next to get a bill through the post."

Tim said, stubbornly "Some of them have paid me, Helen. We need the money."

She whispered "They may have paid once but they'll never have any more to do with us. They say you're even worse than the Jews."

It took a fortnight before Tim got the third reply to his letter: the one from the Lord Mayor. It was a curt reply and cold, and it brought cold hatred to Tim's heart. The Mayor wrote that he had complete confidence in City Councillor Rinkman, and he had let Councillor Rinkman have sight of Tim's letter.

Tim said "Rinkman's seen my letter, Helen. They're all as bad as each other. The whole Council has been corrupted by the Jews."

Helen said nothing, and Tim went on "At least they all know that I mean business."

Tim soon learnt that it wasn't only himself that meant business. A week later a letter arrived from Rinkman and Son, Solicitors, with the threat of a writ for Libel unless Tim withdrew his allegations and made an apology.

Helen was frightened "Take his offer" she said "Withdraw, Tim. Please."

He said "And give in to the Jew? Do you want to see me kicked like a dog?"

She said "He wants you to defend the case; can't you

see? He's trying to provoke you. He wants to get you into his power, like Shylock, and then to twist the knife."

But Tim wasn't listening. In his mind he could picture a High Court and a Judge; the public gallery crowded, and everyone – the Judge, the Jury, the lawyers and the public – held spellbound by oratory. And it was himself, Tim Leston, that he pictured casting the spell: by the force of his words, and by the compulsion of his voice.

He said "You don't need to remind me that I could lose the case, Helen: Libel juries are notoriously unpredictable. But don't you see? Even if I lose I'll have stood-up to him! It will be reported in the newspapers. Everyone will hate the Jew!"

Helen sat silent. At last she managed to say "Is it that important to you, Tim? To fight, even if you lose?"

He said "You were in a wheelchair, Helen. You refused to give-in. That's what he wants, Helen: for us to give-in. To lie-down defeated, below that Jewish Home of his as if it was the Wailing Wall of their Temple." He started to shake; all tensed-up and shaking "I'll destroy his Jewish home just as the Romans destroyed their temple, Helen."

"No!" was all she could say. She knew he was mad enough to do it. He was mad enough to do anything.

"I could do it." he said "I've got friends in the demolition trade. I can get dynamite." His hands twitched again, as if his wiry frame was charged with voltage; like voltage triggering a dynamite charge. "Whatever happens in court" he said "I will have kept my pride against the Jew."

Helen said "It's costs I'm worried about, Tim: Costs of defending an action in the High Court. Daddy's money's nearly all gone, Tim."

He said "We can raise money on the house, on a mortgage. A second mortgage if needs must. And I can cut down on expenses. My Professional Indemnity Insurance, for example. The premiums are outrageous: over a thousand pounds a year, for what? – For nothing! I've never claimed a penny from it."

"I don't understand" she said.

"The policy insures me against claims for negligence" he explained "For bad advice to clients: if a house I'd surveyed were to fall down the next year and that sort of thing. Good surveyors like myself are just subsidising bad surveyors: only a bad surveyor fails to notice dry rot, or damp, or subsidence. The Indemnity Insurance is a confidence trick!"

Helen said "A large mortgage frightens me, Tim. I'm frightened of losing my home... As long as I keep the house I can still feel daddy's strength behind me."

He said "You'll never lose your home, Helen."

She said "I'd die first" and then she said "Can't a Libel case be heard by a Judge in Chambers? Or by a Statutory Chairman, like the case over the Restrictive Covenants?"

He almost laughed at the question "No, Helen. – There's nothing hole-in-the-corner about a Libel case. A Libel case is always big: a Judge and a Jury, and the High Court. It always makes the front page of the newspapers. It's big!"

"Stop!" she said "Please stop, Tim. You're almost enjoying this, aren't you? – You frighten me, Tim. Don't you realise my fear of losing? – My fear of losing everything; the house; everything?"

Once more Tim's hands started to twitch and Helen was reminded of some film she'd once seen: of Boris Karloff as a mechanical monster in human guise, and charged with electricity. Tim's voice came out the same way, as though it had been pre-recorded on some primitive apparatus. "Just think, Helen!" he was saying "Rinkman will never again be able to hide behind respectability. – That's what Jews rely on: on everything being hidden; secret. I'll denounce him in Court, Helen! It will be in all the newspapers. You'll be proud of me."

She said "Don't you have to instruct a Barrister? For the

High Court?"

"I'm entitled to conduct my own defence" he replied "Have you any idea what it costs to brief counsel? Besides, I want to show them all how I can do it myself – It's my big chance, Helen. I could have been great; a great Barrister. To show everyone, Helen! To show the Jews!"

"We can't afford to lose the case" she was whispering though her tears, but her interruption made no more impression on Tim than it would have made on a gramophone record.

"An English Jury will smell corruption" he was saying "I'll show them I could have been a greater lawyer than Gerald Rinkman!"

Helen said "Surely – Gerald Rinkman will brief Counsel, even if you don't?"

Tim said "You may be right.... no... He'll want to fight out in the open, Helen. This is much more than a legal battle... When I joined the Blackshirts, I joined to fight a war. Gerald Rinkman wants to win that war as much as I do. He thinks he's a war hero, don't you see?"

She gave a sort of hopeless smile – it wasn't a smile of happiness, but a smile that was super-imposed on unhappiness. She said "So... between Tim Leston who married me, and Gerald Rinkman who betrayed me, it's to be open war?"

Tim said "I'll be your champion, Helen. I'll slay the dragon." And he added "I'll be in all the newspapers. A great advocate, they'll call me. A great lawyer manqué."

She said "That's more important to you than anything, isn't it? More important than victory? – your pride."

He said "You know, Helen – even if I knew now that I was going to lose, I'd still not miss this chance. Even the greatest lawyer can lose a case. I'll be great, whatever happens. You'll see."

CHAPTER TEN

It was a year before the case came to court.

The Jewish Refugees' Home had long been completed and occupied, and, at least, the terrible building-noises had stopped. But still, there it was, looming over Tim and Helen, and darkening their lives.

Most people would have become used to it, and would have found it no more than an irritation. They might even have come to befriend, or, at least, to tolerate the occupants of the home who were harmless and eager for friendship: they all wore habitual smiles, as if unable to believe their luck to be living in such luxury after the persecution and the pogroms they had endured. But Tim and Helen were immune to sympathy, and guarded their hatred like an eternal flame.

Tim was right: Gerald Rinkman, the Plaintiff, did decide to conduct his own case. It's true, he took Counsel's Opinion: the opinion of an eminent Jewish Q.C., who, predictably, advised him not to conduct his own Case. But Gerald Rinkman chose to ignore his Counsel: it would have been like getting a proxy to fight a duel of honour, with swords.

As for Tim, the Court was for him like the Nuremberg Rally, and he was the leader, the Fuhrer; larger-than-life, and denouncing the enemy. Time after time the Judge had to interrupt him; to rule him out of order, and to instruct the Jury to ignore some preposterous statement that was irrelevant to the Case.

But Tim refused to be silenced: he had the Jury's attention and he knew that some of them secretly sympathised with him – he could tell, by the way they looked at him half admiringly, but warily, all at once.

The public gallery was packed, just as Tim had hoped; there were disturbances, and, once, a scuffle, so that the Judge threatened to clear the court.

Tim's line of defence was to try to prove justification: that what he had written about Gerald was fair comment. But he hardly bothered to present a reasoned argument, and what flowed from his lips was little more than anti-semitic poison. He ignored any thoughts of damages and costs; he was too proud for such inhibitions: the great leaders – the Fuhrer, il Duce, Sir Oswald Mosley – would never have lowered themselves to count the cost in their fight against the Jews. For the first time in his life Tim had the opportunity for greatness, that's how he felt. He was glorious, and people had no choice but to listen to him – it was his moment of glory, and he could feel the invisible presence of the great leaders: the Fuhrer with his power to mesmerise and il Duce who was worshipped like a god. He seemed to hear the crash of a million goose-stepping heels, and a million throats raised in a paean which might have been the Horst Wessel, that paean to the first Nazi martyr, the prototype of the anti-Jew. Or was it a paean to Tim Leston, the only true follower of the Fuhrer who was still dedicated to the fight?

Tim was shouting now, in spite of the Judge, and a Court Official was trying to restrain him. It seemed to Tim that a shadow had come over the court, as if the great eagle of the Third Reich has spread its wings and blocked-out the light.

Tim stopped.

There was silence, and then the Judge was saying "Have you finished?"

Silence again.

Then Gerald Rinkman was addressing the Jury, and he was like a man alone, speaking empty words into emptiness. Gerald wanted the Jury's hearts, but all he got from them was a blank stare; not exactly a hostile stare, but a stare devoid of all sympathy; a stare of heartless indifference like the stares of those onlookers who were photographed standing aside while the Nazis were herding Jews into cattle-trucks and away to death.

The Judge summed-up, and directed the Jury.

The Jury did their duty, and found for the plaintiff: for Gerald Rinkman, the Jew. How could they have found otherwise?

But the damages that the Jury awarded were trifling: a mere hundred pounds. There would be costs of course, which would make it hurt for Tim, but that would be later. For now, for a brief moment, it was a sort of triumph.

There were headlines in the newspapers and photographs: the Liverpool Echo and the Liverpool Daily Post made it a sensation. There was a photograph of Tim on the front page: he was shown as the villain, of course, who'd dared to utter a Libel against a Jew, and, what's more, had tried to justify the Libel in court. Everyone still felt a sort of collective guilt over what had happened to the Jews in the war. But, in a strange way, Tim wasn't simply seen as a villain: in the same way that Dick Turpin, for instance, was both a villain and a hero, all at once. For the first time in his life Tim the anonymous, Tim the obscure, was pointed-out in the street; and most of the looks he got were looks of admiration. Tim walked taller: for the first time in his life he was somebody; and Colonel Gerald Rinkman, M.C. the war hero, was suddenly vulnerable.

"I lost" Tim announced to Helen "But, somehow, I feel I've won."

She'd not gone to Court. She'd found she couldn't face it: couldn't face Gerald Rinkman, all smug and confident and certain to win; Gerald Rinkman who'd taken the winnings and left her the loser, like a dog that's left to die in a ditch.

Tim's bravado didn't cheer her. "You lost" she said "How do you mean – you feel you've won?"

He tried to explain "A Libel Jury assesses the damages.

Sometimes they award only token damages – it used to be a halfpenny. – Really, if that happens it's the so-called winner who's mocked."

"Was Gerald Rinkman mocked?" she asked.

"Mocked?" he echoed "Damages of a paltry hundred-pounds? – There's a name for such damages, Helen. Derisory! Derisory Damages. Gerald's the one who's derided."

"And costs?" she said "Costs, Tim?"

"Well!" he tried to bluster "Costs, yes. – Perhaps three-thousand? It's worth it, Helen! It's worth it, to see Gerald Rinkman derided!"

She tried to smile, but her face only twitched. It was her nerves again. Her nerves were always letting her down these days. And the Jewish Home was always there. Whatever Tim said about Rinkman being derided, Rinkman's Home was always there deriding herself and Tim.

She said "I keep telling you that daddy's money's running-out Tim. All that extravagance – and now, these costs!"

But he wasn't listening. He was hearing the sound of Nuremberg and a million voices shouting "Sieg Heil!" He said "I wish you'd been there in Court, Helen... When I denounced the Jew... the Judge kept interrupting, but I wouldn't be silenced... I took my inspiration from Shakespeare, you know: from Portia denouncing Shylock the Jew. I could see that the Jury was impressed... everyone was impressed."

There was a noise at the front door, of the evening newspaper coming through the letterbox. Tim hurried to fetch it "Here it is, Helen!" he shouted "On the front page: a photograph of me; and one of the Jew. You can see he's cunning, Helen."

"Cunning as Shylock" she said.

"He didn't get his pound of flesh!" Tim's voice was triumphant. "Oh, how he tried, Helen! How he feigned modesty. How hesitant and humble he was. Not like the real Gerald Rinkman at all. Since when was Gerald Rinkman humble? Oh, hypocrite Jew! – The proud Jew, pretending to be humble, to get his pound of flesh."

"Remember the costs, Tim." Helen said "Gerald may not have got his pound of flesh, but the costs may be enough to tear-out our heart."

"It's worth the costs" he replied "The public gallery was packed, Helen. Everyone was on my side, I could feel it. Sir Oswald Mosley should have been there; he'd have been proud... All the time, I've been fighting for Mosley, you know.... when I denounced the Jew!... When I warned everyone in court about the Jews. I modelled myself on Mosley, Helen... It might have been our great leader himself that was speaking... Oh, what I'd have given to have been wearing my Blackshirt uniform!... They even started to clap, Helen; people in the public gallery... until the Judge called for silence and threatened to clear the Court."

Helen was almost convinced that it had been a sort of triumph. She said "Gerald Rinkman can never be complacent again... the war-hero... the Colonel... he'll be looking over his shoulder at all those people in the public gallery... he'll never feel safe."

Tim said "The way he treated you, Helen... it's a kind of revenge; a kind of justice."

She said "If only we didn't need to worry about money, Tim! I'll never feel safe while Gerald Rinkman's after his pound of flesh. He'll never give-up now, unless he gets his pound of flesh."

Tim went to the cupboard where he kept his most precious things: his album of newspaper cuttings and his photographs. There was the cutting from The Times of June the 8th, 1934, of the great rally at Olympia the previous evening. Oh, the memories it brought-back, and the pride! The way the Blackshirt stewards had kicked-out the Reds! No half-measures – the boot! And, when some dirty Reds had got-up, somehow, into the roof-space and started throwing things, how the Blackshirts had made the Reds pay for it! Even the Blackshirt girls were trying to scratch their shifty-Red eyes out! Tim said "There were girl Blackshirts... I wish you could have been a Blackshirt, Helen, rather than a cripple."

And here was the photograph cut-out from the London Evening News, of Sir Oswald inspecting his men. He was all dressed-up in the latest uniform, just before uniforms were banned by law: you could tell from the way the riding-britches were grey rather than black, and by the red-and-white armband of the British Union with the lightning-flash. The photograph made Tim proud and angry all at once: proud of Sir Oswald, looking so splendid in his high boots and peaked cap; with his arm thrust forward in the Fascist salute, and his intense, mesmeric eyes. Yet ashamed, too; ashamed to remember that the inspection had been made after Sir Oswald had capitulated to the Reds, and had marched his men away from Cable Street rather than fight. And there, in the front rank of the photograph, with a stare as intense as that of his leader, stood Tim in full uniform. "Remember this?" he said "I'll always keep today's newspaper together with these."

"It's been such a long fight" she said "Against Gerald Rinkman. Has it been worth it, Tim?"

He said "That old photograph... that uniform is what gave us heart, Helen. It's what kept you alive."

She felt once more the old bitterness, and the impotent longing to hit-back; to get revenge for what she'd been made to suffer. She said "After all the pain – I could never love any man but a Blackshirt, Tim."

He went upstairs, and she waited; remembering everything and waiting.

Tim didn't stop at the first landing; he went on, up; up

to the attic, and to the wardrobe of which only he had the key. The wardrobe door creaked when he opened it, and there was a heavy scent of mothballs; but, inside, everything was just as he'd left it: the black shirt, and cap, and tunic; the high boots and leather belt, both still shiny under the dust: the uniform of an officer of the British Union of Fascists; a paramilitary uniform that had been forbidden by Law since 1936.

The mere sight of the uniform made Tim thrust back his bony shoulders. Quickly he took-off his ordinary suit and his conventional tie, and there he was, soon, reflected in the mirror: all black and magnificent; the scourge of the Jews.

He had climbed the stairs in the manner of a Chartered Surveyor with hardly a creak; but he came down loudly, like a Blackshirt, with heavy tread. On the lower landing he paused, beside the mirror on the wall. He stared intently into the mirror, and into the reflection that met him there. Then, suddenly, he clicked his heels, and thrust his arm in the Fascist salute. "Sieg Heil!" he shouted; and Helen heard him stamping down the lower flight of stairs. "Oh, Tim!" she said "My Blackshirt!"

Tim felt masterful, in a way that he rarely felt: one of the Master Race. Hitler was dead, and Mosley would die some day soon, but Fascism would live forever, as long as there were Jews.

He stood in his splendour before her, and she said "I found you so attractive, Tim, the first time I saw you in your uniform." – She was remembering how the Blackshirt uniform had been something for her to worship, and to take the place of the way she had worshipped Gerald Rinkman. Tim had always been so masterful in his uniform, and so unlike the Tim she'd first known, who had been her slave.

Before her accident, when she'd been the queen, she'd taken Tim for granted. Then, afterwards, when he'd saved her from despair, and married her, she still needed him as her slave; only when he was making love to her did she close her eyes and pretend he was the master. It had been so awkward, making love, in their first years of marriage: they had to arrange themselves, carefully, so as not to hurt her, and it could never be spontaneous. She would never have a child, because of her injuries, they had told her that. Tim had accepted it, like he'd accepted everything.

Even then, after all that; after all that pain – even then, when, Oh! so gentle and concerned about her, and so considerate, Tim had entered her and made love to her; even then, secretly, when she closed her eyes, it was Gerald there, in her mind – Gerald Rinkman whom she hated; Gerald, who'd dumped her like a dead dog in a ditch. It was still Gerald that she secretly wanted, and the hard, selfish, wonderful sex of him: all the while that Tim was being Oh! so gentle and considerate to his poor, crippled wife, Helen had yearned for that.

How she hated Gerald Rinkman! And yet she yearned for him. And then – that day came when Tim put on his uniform, all black and with shining–leather! Then; then! when he'd been oh! so masterful: the Blackshirt officer; and oh! so apologetic afterwards and worried in case he'd hurt her. Only then, for the first time, did she open her eyes to him; and, when she felt the thrust – when she felt the hard thrust of him – every thrust had been a bayonet-thrust, stabbing at the memory of Gerald Rinkman whom she hated.

And, now, Tim was here again facing her in his uniform. And there it was, through his open trousers; the hard, curved bayonet ready to thrust, to thrust into her, and deep into the hated heart of Gerald Rinkman, the Jew.

"Now!" she was saying "Now! Like that first time! The way you hurt me then, and it was so wonderful, I didn't care."

"Sieg Heil!" he shouted and "Now!" she shouted back at him "Now!"

"Wait!" he ordered, and went to the gramophone. He selected a record of his favourite Wagner, and turned-up the volume so that the music from Valhalla crashed around them like a thunderstorm. Then, like Siegfried, he went to her; like a storm-trooper he invaded her; and, like a Teutonic Knight, he put her to the sword. All around him crashed the music, and, in his mind, he was seeing, not the decor of a suburban drawing-room, but rolling clouds and clashing steel. Other images, too, came racing through his mind; images from wartime newsreels, and the images of his own imagination, all confused: of screaming Stuka divebombers, and bombs like giant penises penetrating the earth: of a column of great black tanks, Panzers, and every tank with its death's-head S.S. emblem; each with its gun thrusting forward like a Fascist salute and ready to rape: of Heidelberg Students, each with his scar of honour and with his sabre thrust-forward – On guard!: of Nazis bawling their heads off in a Bier-Keller and stamping through Munich, singing about Horst Wessel who died for the Cause: of men and women, and children too, all screaming in terror as the gas poured into the gas-chamber.... and every tortured, terrified face that Tim saw was the face of Gerald Rinkman... and the pitiless face of the Camp guard who opened the gas-taps was the face of Tim Leston the Blackshirt, Sir Oswald Mosley's man.

Tim loosed his belt and attacked! Lunge and lunge and lunge again! – He'd not have cared if he'd drawn blood, in the way that the students are indifferent to blood at Heidelberg.

Helen was watching him, and, when he lunged, she shuddered with the violence of it. But, when he lunged his last, she shuddered not in pain, but in ecstasy. And all the pain inside her that she always felt, that never, ever, left her, was, for a moment, assuaged.

Tim stood-up, and turned-off the music.

"You were wonderful" Helen said "In your uniform."

He'd never worn the uniform, all during the war; he couldn't have risked being interned like Mosley. Besides, there had been something else that he couldn't explain, even to himself: something about being ashamed, and not really knowing whose side he was on, during the war.

As for Helen, she was remembering all the disappointments on those other occasions, when Tim had made love to her with so much consideration because of her injuries and she'd tried to stop herself wishing it was Gerald Rinkman whom she hated. But this time it had been wonderful, wonderful, with the S.S. dagger stabbing; with the sword and bayonet thrusting; with the Panzer guns and Stuka bombs penetrating, and destroying the memory of the Jew.

"You were wonderful, Tim." she said again.

He replied "I wish you could have seen me in Court, Helen. When I denounced the Jew! Even though I say it myself, Helen, I held them all spellbound. How I wish I'd been able to wear this uniform!"

"I wish you'd wear it more often, Tim" she said "I want you to wear it for me."

His voice was raised in anger when he answered "They banned the uniform in 'thirty-six. It was the Jews again, Helen; the old conspiracy... The Jews control everything: the Law, the Government, the newspapers; everything. Hitler knew all about it, Helen."

She said "Hitler went too far, Tim... the Gas-Chambers... the experiments on those poor people..." She still couldn't bear to feel the guilt of her own hatred of Jews.

He said "When the Government banned the Blackshirt uniform, I felt betrayed. We were the greatest patriots, Helen: our flag was the Union Flag. A threat to the British Constitution, they said we were! – only the Jews could have twisted the truth like that! Only Jewish newspapers could have made people believe it – I tell you: our great leader Mosley, the greatest patriot in Britain, was betrayed."

He was remembering the humiliation: how they'd interned Sir Oswald and his wife during the war: the great leader humiliated and digging his own potatoes, and peeling them himself in a prison yard. And he was remembering all the servicemen in uniform, khaki or blue: millions of them; and Gerald Rinkman the war-hero, a Colonel, dressed-up in Service Dress with his M.C. and his Sam-Browne belt – while he, Tim Leston had no clothing coupons even to buy himself a new shirt, and was reduced to skulking shabbily about Liverpool, trying not to be noticed. If he'd dared to go out dressed in a Blackshirt uniform he might have been lynched, or, at the very least, arrested and interned like Mosley. Or, even worse, all the heroes in khaki and blue would have pointed their fingers and derided him.

He tried to put these memories out of his mind. He said "The war's over, Helen, and we've still got the Jews in England. The Blackshirt uniform is a reminder of that. I'll wear the uniform secretly, just for you."

"I'd like that, Tim." she said "It makes me so excited, to see you in your uniform."

CHAPTER ELEVEN

The hundred-pounds Damages might have been thought derisory, but it was the Costs that hurt. If he'd allowed himself, Tim might have reflected that, despite the derisory damages, Gerald Rinkman was probably satisfied with the way the Costs would cut Tim. If it wasn't, quite, a pound of flesh from the heart, it was a cut as keen as a sabre-slash.

When Helen was told how high the Costs actually were she was aghast, and all her old nervousness came back. "We'll lose the house, Tim" she kept saying "I'd die if I had to leave this house. It was daddy's house, you see."

Tim smiled indulgently "Don't worry" he said "Trust me."

But she wasn't convinced, and, why should she trust him now, when all he'd ever done was to feed off her inheritance like a vampire? Oh! how she'd wanted Tim to be big; to be as big, and as important as Gerald Rinkman. That's why she'd let him suck the life-blood from her inheritance like a vampire. At first, she'd expected Tim's business to prosper, and for him to revitalise her fortune, like a blood-donor. But such hopes were short-lived. She'd known quite soon that Tim – her husband, Tim – would never be a success; would never be a hero like Gerald Rinkman. But she'd let him carry-on, sucking her inheritance dry, to pay for the office, and the car, and for all the prestige. If it hadn't been for the war, and the false prosperity it had brought them because Tim's rivals had been called-up, disaster would have struck much earlier.

She said "There's no money left, Tim. You'll have to cut-down: get a smaller office, and a smaller car."

"How Gerald Rinkman will love that!" Tim sneered "Do you really want Gerald Rinkman to crow?" He knew she was vulnerable, more vulnerable than himself, about prestige, and he pressed the point "We'll keep-up appearances, Helen.

We must. I'll cut the Costs that don't show. And we can increase the mortgage on the house."

"No" she said "No, Tim."

"We've no choice" he replied "Unless you want Gerald Rinkman to win."

"What are these costs that don't show?" she asked.

"I thought I told you – there's my Professional Indemnity Insurance. The Premiums are outrageous, Helen. Thousands a year! It's just a subsidy for bad surveyors. Let me explain: a poor surveyor does a careless job and he's sued for damages by his client. But it's the Insurance that pays."

Helen was so shocked she could hardly speak "You can't give the Insurance up, Tim! I'd never sleep for worry if you gave it up."

He was angry "The good surveyors – the real professionals, like myself – surveyors who always give sound advice; we're penalised. We pay high Insurance Premiums, and the incompetent surveyors collect."

She said "We'd lose everything, Tim, if you were to be sued, and lost."

But Tim wasn't listening; he was saying "While we're on the subject of my business, there's another thing: the importance of personal recommendation. All the professions – lawyers, accountants, surveyors – we all depend on personal recommendation. I should be able to depend on your friends to be my clients."

"Oh, Tim!" she exclaimed; but she couldn't go on. She'd lost so many friends already because of Tim, and how could she tell him? She'd been so popular, all those years ago, before her terrible accident. She'd never been near the tennis club since; she couldn't have borne it: to see everyone else having fun. She'd been so popular, and not just with the men; she'd had lots of girl friends too. She'd never been one of those girls who only bother with men. Then, after the accident, when

Gerald had dropped her, like a dead dog in a ditch, none of the other men even took the trouble to visit her, except for Tim of course. But, at first, her girl-friends did bother about her; not all of them, but all the loyal ones. Some of the girls were only false friends, but others would have been loyal, but for Tim; lots of girls felt creepy about Tim. But still there was a loyal core of best friends who had never deserted her, in spite of Tim. That's what made her want to protest now, but she couldn't say why; because Tim was her husband, and she had to stay loyal to him.

It was the way he always tried to make use of friends, that made Tim unattractive to so many people, Helen was thinking – it must have been something missing in him; an emotional emptiness, or something.

"Your friends should be glad to be my clients" Tim repeated, and Helen said "Oh, Tim! If only you didn't come across as so obsessive! – My friends all say you're paranoid against Jews. It embarrasses them, so they don't visit me. All Jews aren't like Gerald Rinkman, Tim."

He was still angry. "What sort of friends are they?" he said "Can't they understand how badly you've been treated by a Jew?"

She said "It's unfashionable to be anti-Semitic. Before the war the Jews weren't popular, but everybody sympathises with the Jews now, after the gas-chambers."

He snapped "It's our duty to warn people. If we all give-in to Rinkman and his friends we're lost."

She said "It's not only the way you go-on about Jews, Tim; as I've already told you – my friends don't like the way you try to take advantage of their friendship to get business. They're still saying it's rather Jewish of you, Tim. That's only a joke, but there's a sting in it."

He was really angry now "With friends like that you don't need enemies, Helen" he shouted.

She'd been through it all before, but she might as well never have said it. He'd chosen to ignore it, and put it out of his mind, as he always ignored criticism. She knew that it was hopeless, and that he'd take no more notice now, but still, she had to say it again, as a protest; to show how much it hurt her, to lose her friends.

She tried to explain, without provoking him, but it was impossible. She said, and it was like replaying an old record "Someone starts talking about their home – everyone's always talking about houses: about how they might have dry-rot or something. Then you join-in, and make a joke about the man whose legs came through the ceiling because of dry-rot in the floor above. Everyone laughs at the joke – until you send out a bill for professional advice on dry-rot! No wonder I lose my friends, Tim."

"Advice is valuable" he interrupted. But Helen went-on. She'd been trying to bring herself to speak-out on the subject for years, but now that she'd breached the dyke once it all came flooding out again. "If someone's thinking of buying a house, or selling, they've only got to mention it vaguely, and you're on to it. You say you'd like to help them; how you can find a buyer for them. Or, if they want to buy, you always know the right house for them, a jewel. They think you're helping them, out of kindness – until they get your bill!"

Tim was defensive, and still angry "What can they expect? Free advice? – Professional advice is valuable." But he wasn't as obtuse as he was pretending; he knew very well there was truth in what she was saying, and why he did it: it was all those overheads, the grand office and everything, and not enough business to keep it all going.

"Don't you see, Tim?" she said "My friends never actually approach you professionally. You presume on their friendship and they feel exploited. They pay your bill, of course, but they never come back. They're too frightened it will happen again."

He said "If they really were good friends, they'd want my professional advice, and be glad to pay."

She was exasperated "People aren't like that, Tim. Soon, I'll have no friends left. If it wasn't for Pat Curry, my best and oldest friend, I don't know what I'd do."

Right from the start, after the accident, when Helen was wishing she'd died – before even Tim had come back to her – there'd always been Pat Curry. Helen couldn't remember a time when Pat hadn't been there, as close and as unobtrusive as Helen's own shadow: at school, then at the tennis club when Helen had always been on centre-court with everybody watching her, while Pat was always behind the tea-cups. Not that Pat was plain: she was quite pretty, with a nice smile; but she wasn't popular like Helen. People liked Pat, but they didn't take much notice of her; she helped with the teas, and played the occasional set of tennis with other girls. She wasn't often asked to make-up a mixed doubles.

Only after the accident did Helen appreciate how much she'd always relied on Pat, and taken her for granted. If it hadn't been for Pat, she'd have had few visitors, but Pat rallied the other girls round just when Helen needed girl-friends more than anything.

There'd been all those girl-friends, but, over the years, one by one they'd fallen away; and it was Tim that had done it: Tim with his anti-Semitic rantings that got worse and worse, so that everyone who heard him felt embarrassed and wanted to escape. And then, as if that wasn't bad enough, Tim trapped them into paying him money, the way a spider traps its victims, with words as sticky and as innocent-sounding as gossamer.

Helen said, quietly "Promise me, Tim, that you'll never do anything like that to Pat. You'll never ask Pat for money."

He forced a laugh "Trust me, dear" he said. But how could she trust him? Should she ever have trusted him?

She said, and her voice was so quiet he hardly heard her
"I've overheard people talking – they pretended they didn't
know I was there, but, really, they wanted me to overhear.
They say that you must be partly Jewish Tim: to protest so
violently against Jews, and then to act like a Jew, yourself."

"How dare you, Helen?" he shouted. She'd never seen
him like this, so out of control and violent. She cowered as if
expecting a blow.

She said "Your grandmother Rebecca: she was Rebecca
Ziegler before she married."

"How do you know that?" he hissed. He'd always been
careful to keep the name secret.

"I was tidying your cupboards" she said "Those old
papers from your parents' home. I found your grandparents'
marriage certificate."

"Snooping!" he shouted; and this time he really did
raise his hand. It made her panic "Don't!" she begged "Please,
Tim. Remember how I'm crippled."

He lowered his hand, and his face crumpled, almost to
tears. At last he spoke "Never tell anyone, Helen. Never."
After a long pause, he whispered "Hitler's grandfather was
probably a Jew – it's uncertain because Hitler's father was
illegitimate."

Helen said "The Jews have suffered enough under
Hitler, Tim. Please – let us try to forget the Jews."

Tim said "Gerald Rinkman's a Jew, Helen. We can't get
away from that."

"If I can make myself forget Gerald Rinkman, after all
I've suffered – surely you can forget him too, Tim?"

He said "Gerald Rinkman will never allow us to forget
him, Helen. After the Libel case, and those derisory damages,
he'll never be satisfied. He'll still want his pound of flesh."

She said "What of the Costs against us? Those terrible
Costs? – Surely that will satisfy him, Tim?"

He said "It isn't only money, Helen. If there's one thing that Jews love even more than money Helen, it's face. Those derisory damages, Helen – Gerald Rinkman's been publicly derided. He'll want his pound of flesh for that." He was regaining his confidence, with the memory of his finest hour: when he'd stood-up in Court and everybody had had to listen. When he'd held the stage, and denounced the Jews. Oh, how his old leader Sir Oswald Mosley would have been proud of him, to hear the way he'd denounced the Jews! He said "I would have been a great lawyer, Helen, if it hadn't been for Gerald Rinkman. I want my pound of flesh as much as he does."

She said "I'm frightened, Tim. In trying to destroy Gerald Rinkman you could destroy yourself. You'll destroy me, too, Tim. We'll all be destroyed."

His reply was cold "Perhaps that's the price we'll have to pay." There was a look of mad obstinacy on his face that frightened her, for it reminded her of the old newsreels at the time of Nuremberg, and the mad face of Hitler at the Rally.

Next day, when Tim was out, Pat Curry came to visit. Pat was always a comfort; she'd never changed in the way she treated Helen, as if she was still grateful for Helen to notice her. Pat came in her little car; she came, as usual, in time for afternoon tea, when Tim was unlikely to be home from the office.

Pat had never married; she was a teacher, and had come straight from afternoon lessons at the school where she taught, with a pile of exercise-books on the back seat of her car, as an excuse for her not to stay too long. The real reason was that she wanted to be away before Tim got home – Helen knew that, and Pat knew that she knew, but the exercise-books smoothed it over.

Pat was still quite pretty, and people – women – used to wonder why she'd never married. She'd have made a good wife, but no man had ever seemed to notice.

Pat was feeling really bubbly – she was nearly always bubbly, like Bubbles in the soap advertisement. She had something to be bubbly about, and she couldn't wait to tell Helen.

She knew she had to be careful; because of Tim. What she was bubbly about was the sort of thing that would make Tim want to catch the bubbles for himself, and to burst them and spoil everything. But she couldn't bottle-up the bubbles any more – she'd make Helen promise not to tell; and Helen wouldn't dare to break the promise because of all the friends she'd already lost. Pat's bubbly secret that she couldn't bottle-up was that, at last, she'd found the cottage she'd always dreamed about.

Not long ago, Pat's mother had died, after years of depending on Pat: one of the reasons, perhaps, for men not noticing her. So now, at last, Pat could sell the old house, that was dark as death, and move to the cottage of her dreams, that was full of light. She had brought the Estate Agent's particulars with her, and she made the mistake of leaving them open, on the back-seat of her car, beside the exercise-books.

Helen had started to make the tea when Pat arrived, so Pat helped. Helen said "What would I do without you, Pat? – You've heard about Tim? He lost the Libel case to Gerald Rinkman."

Pat said "Chin up! What's a hundred pounds? That's as good as a victory for you."

Helen said "But, the Costs!"

Pat said "If it comes to the worst, I might be able to help. Mother left me a nest-egg, you know."

Helen said "Pat, you're my best friend – but I couldn't."

Late sunlight was coming through the french-windows like a beam of hope. Really, now that the Jewish building work was finished, it wasn't all that bad; if it hadn't been an eternal reminder of Gerald Rinkman getting his own way.

Pat said "And now I've some news. But, first, you must promise not to tell anyone. Not even Tim."

Helen said "If it's Tim you're worried about... I don't want to lose my best friend. I'd never risk losing you, Pat."

"Guess what?" said Pat "Now that I've got some money, I'm thinking of moving to that cottage in Woolton village that I've coveted for years."

Helen said "I didn't know it was up for sale."

Pat said "The Agent is Sykes-Waterhouse. I took a copy of the particulars. I'll put in an offer right away."

Helen said "Sykes-Waterhouse – that's Tim's favourite Estate Agent. He often does surveys for them. Will you put-in an offer without a survey? – Is that wise?"

Pat bubbled-on "I can't wait – I couldn't bear anyone else to get the cottage. I've set my heart on it. It's symbolic, somehow, to me. A symbol of light in my life."

There was the sound of a car in the drive, and of the key turning in the front door. It was Tim, home early.

Pat changed the subject from the cottage, but she was still bubbly. She said "Tim. How pretty this house is! – The sunshine and the garden. I've always envied you your garden."

Tim didn't smile. He said "That building overlooking us and the damned Jews! – It's an outrage! It's ruined the garden for me."

Pat said "You don't know how lucky you are. Anyone would be proud of this house; and this garden." She was trying to smooth things over. It was what she'd always been good at: smoothing things over.

Tim said "You've always liked this house for its light, compared with your mother's dark house. Is that why you're interested in the Woolton cottage?"

Pat caught her breath, and she didn't look bubbly any more. She glanced nervously at Helen, who was trying to smile.

Tim said "They told me at Sykes-Waterhouse that there was somebody interested. They always keep me well-informed you know. Then I saw the particulars on the back-seat of your car and I knew it was you."

Pat tried to change the subject, and, to flatter him, she said "I've heard all about the impression you made in Court, Tim. The way you handled your own case. People were impressed."

Tim smiled his thin smile "Masterful, is what they called it. Yes, Pat, I could have been a masterful lawyer. But I chose to master the profession of surveyor. You'll need a master-surveyor, Pat."

"Oh!" she knew she'd laid herself open to checkmate like a chess-player who fails to protect her king.

She said "I've decided not to have a survey, Tim. I'm so in-love with the cottage – I'm like a lover, prepared to overlook every fault."

"You must have a survey, even so," he said "You love the cottage, so you'll want it to stand for ever... An old cottage is bound to have structural problems. Before you move-in is the best time to put things right."

"What kind of problems do you mean?" she said. She was less bubbly, and was starting to feel worried, as Tim had intended.

"I've discussed the property at Sykes-Waterhouse" he said "With the manager of course: I always go straight to the top. I'm afraid there are problems, Pat. You'll certainly need to instruct a surveyor."

Pat gave-in; her bubbles had burst and vanished. "You, Tim?" she asked.

For the first time, Tim's thin smile had some warmth in it "You couldn't find a better surveyor, Pat" he said "A master, though I say it myself."

Helen had been sitting silent, and getting more and more tense; unable to intervene in the inevitable sequence of events that would, she knew, lead ultimately to her losing her last and dearest friend. She tried, now, impotently to intervene. "Tim" she said "Business between friends is never a good idea."

"On the contrary, my dear" he replied "I wouldn't like to think of an old friend like Pat in the hands of any other surveyor but myself. I'd worry that she'd be let-down."

Tim had made no attempt to sit-down, ever since he came in. He remained standing, and his expansive gestures seemed compelling, even from such a small man. Helen knew she had no chance of discouraging him: business had been slow, and Tim needed all the business he could get. He said "Another thing, Pat: the house you're living-in now – the house you were fortunate enough to inherit from your mother – will you be selling it through Sykes-Waterhouse?"

Pat was guarded in her reply, but she was as defenceless as a guard who, without a weapon, confronts an adversary armed with poisoned steel. "I'll try to sell the house myself," she said "To save the Agent's Commission."

Tim feigned enthusiasm for the plan. "What a good idea!" he said, then, after a theatrical pause, he added "Unfortunately it's rarely successful. But, you can have the best of both worlds – get Sykes-Waterhouse to agree to a sale-only Commission; then, if you do manage to sell the house yourself, you'll pay them nothing."

Pat couldn't see any catch in it: perhaps Tim really was trying to help her; and the bubbles began to surface once again.

"I tell you what" Tim went on – he was talking fast, now, so she'd catch his enthusiasm "Let me do it all for you. Let me place the particulars of your present property with Sykes-Waterhouse."

Once more, Pat smelt danger "Oh, no!" she interrupted

"I couldn't do that, Tim." And Helen, too, was saying "No, Tim. – Tim and Pat. No; please."

Tim carried on, oblivious. "I'd be delighted to help – and you'd be doing me a favour in return, Pat; at no cost to yourself. Let me explain: when surveyors like myself introduce a Client to an Estate Agent, the Agent pays us one third of the Commission of the completed sale. It's standard practice. You'd be helping me, Pat, and so you'd be helping Helen. How can you lose?"

Pat said "But, if I do manage to sell privately? – there'd be no Agent's fee for you to share."

"Well, of course," Tim reassured her "In the unlikely event of a private sale, I wouldn't expect anything."

Pat rose to leave, and Tim accompanied her to her car. He said "It's lucky you left the Estate Agent's particulars on the back seat. I might never have known that it was you who was after the cottage."

Helen stayed indoors. She had hardly been able to force a smile of goodbye. She was in the grip of a kind of anger, as powerful as the anger she felt whenever she thought of Gerald Rinkman; but this was a different kind of anger, cold and with no passion in it – an anger against Tim, that made her despise him, and made her despise herself for marrying a man as mean as he.

When Tim came back, Helen spoke bitterly "You promised never to do anything like that to Pat. You never keep your promises, Tim."

"I'm doing Pat a favour" Tim replied, and he was so smug and insufferable Helen wanted to scream. "She'll have the best surveyor in Liverpool" he went on "That cottage will need a lot of attention."

Next morning, early, before she'd be on her way to school, Tim telephoned Pat, and asked her what selling-price she had in mind, for her house. She told him she'd already placed a private advertisement in the newspaper, and the price that she was hoping for, though she'd decided not to stipulate a price in the advertisement. It was more or less the valuation Tim would have made himself. He didn't need to visit the house; he knew it well from memory. He knew so many houses from memory, the details of which were all filed away in his mind.

He drove to Sykes-Waterhouse, and he was shown straight in to the manager; they knew how to flatter him. Next day, Pat's property was featured, as part of Sykes-Waterhouse's large advertisement, in the Liverpool Daily Post.

Tim asked the manager for the keys of the Woolton Cottage, and carried-out his survey the same day. It was a pretty cottage, and Tim began to feel resentful that a woman like Pat Curry could afford to buy it, and without a mortgage too. He might not have felt so resentful if things were still the same for him as they had been when Helen's father died, and they'd been flush with money and with an un-mortgaged house. But now, when he was in debt, and with such a large mortgage that he'd had to give-up his Professional Indemnity Insurance to pay the interest, he felt that people like Pat had no right to good fortune, and that he, Tim Leston, had a right to his share.

He could so easily have carried-out a thorough survey – he was a good surveyor – but, perversely, he couldn't bring himself to do it; he couldn't bear to give value for money when he felt so resentful. He made a cursory tour of the cottage, inside and outside; he poked his head into the loft, looked at the wiring, and checked for damp and rot. It barely took him half an hour, but he found enough that needed attention to make his bill and his report seem plausible. Then he went away and typed-out a bill for a Full Structural Survey, with a thumping fee.

Pat had prepared herself for a shock – she knew Tim's reputation, and the way he'd exploited Helen's other friends.

She knew she'd left herself open, but, when the bill came, it was far more than she'd expected. It was outrageous, and she knew she'd been trapped – she'd gone into it expecting to be trapped, and knowing that, if she refused to enter the trap her friendship with Helen would be over. She found herself starting to hate Helen, and starting to cry. She'd refuse to pay the bill! She was about to pick-up the 'phone, when she had second-thoughts.

Bubbly as she usually was – though not bubbly now – and with all the efforts she'd always made to be liked, serving behind the teacups and everything; despite all these efforts, the only real friend she'd ever had, her first and best friend, was Helen Pringle who now was Helen Leston.

She still had tears in her eyes as she wrote-out a cheque and put it into an envelope, to post to Tim.

When Tim opened the envelope he smiled. The money would tide them over.

A few days later, he called into Sykes-Waterhouse and the manager told him that Pat's mother's house had been sold; but not to a client of Sykes-Waterhouse – it had been a private sale. The manager didn't seem unduly distressed, and might even have been feeling a secret smugness. He'd always resented having to share his Agent's hard-earned fee with a surveyor who'd done no more than act as a middle-man.

"You'll be interested to know" the manager added "Now that she's sold her present house, Miss Curry has made a firm offer for the Woolton Cottage."

Tim walked out of the Estate Agency feeling angry with the world, and the way it was treating him. He felt an irrational need for vengeance, or, at least, the need to redress the balance; to get his own back on everyone who'd ever got the better of him. If that couldn't, yet, be Gerald Rinkman, then it would have to be someone else, someone weak: Pat Curry; yes, Pat who'd profited at his expense, and sold her house privately so he couldn't get his share of the Agent's Fee.

The pressures of everything that had happened to him – and the way he'd always been a loser, – had already twisted his mind. In his twisted way, he now saw Pat as someone who'd cheated him out of his rightful fee, by going behind his back, and selling privately.

He went home, and took out the portable typewriter, that he had to make do with, now that he could no longer afford an office and a secretary – not that he'd ever, really, been able to afford them, out of the fees he earned. An office and a secretary had been essential for Tim to look as big as Gerald Rinkman; and it was Rinkman, the dirty Jew, who'd bled Helen of her inheritance.

Tim had never learned to type properly, and Gerald Rinkman must never suspect that he was reduced to doing his own typing. So he hit each key slowly and deliberately; and the force of each letter-key as it struck the paper felt like his fist striking out at all the enemies who had conspired to do him down. He knew Sykes-Waterhouse's standard scale of charges for a house-sale: one and a half percent, and he assumed that Pat Curry had got her asking price for the house. So he made out a bill for half of one percent of the asking price (one third of one and a half percent) and he posted the bill to Pat.

When Pat got the bill, she felt sick, resentful, angry; all at once. She'd been so pleased at herself for achieving a private sale. It was a little triumph in her life. Now this spoilt everything, and put a shadow over everything, even over the anticipation of moving into her cottage.

After the first bill, the one for the survey, she'd bit her lip, and not mentioned it to Helen. She'd paid the bill, and it had hurt to pay it, but, at least, she'd been paying for something positive, or so she believed: for Tim's time and for his expert opinion; and she had the comfort that her precious jewel, her cottage, had been thoroughly checked-over and surveyed.

But, now, – this! As his part in selling the house, Tim had done nothing! – Nothing! And he'd promised – even Helen had heard him promise – that there was no question of his asking for a fee if she made a private sale. That's what made it all the more hurtful: she'd thought she was doing it as a favour for a friend – he'd asked it as a favour from a friend – and how could she have refused, when it seemed to cost her nothing?

If the Estate Agents had made the sale, she'd have willingly paid their fee, and Tim's cut of the fee would have cost her nothing. Except that it wasn't quite so simple as that. She hadn't liked to say so at the time; and, oh! how she wished now that she'd had the courage to say it, but, surely, Sykes-Waterhouse would have had less incentive to sell the house if they knew they'd lose a third of their fee?

She found she could not bear to pay this latest bill; at least, not without a protest. She had to make a protest, for her own sake; she had to put her own feelings before Helen's feelings, just for once.

It took a lot of courage, but she drove to Helen's house, and rang the bell. Tim opened the door and pretended to be pleased to see her. He said "Pat! – Helen will be delighted that you've called. I'll make tea."

"Wait!" she said, fearing that her determination would vanish if she delayed "I've something to say to you, Tim. To Helen, too."

Helen had come into the entrance hall, and Pat said "Hello Helen. I've sold mother's house – I sold it myself. And now Tim's sent me a bill for his cut of an imaginary Agent's Fee."

Helen was standing there, and the shock of Pat's voice raised in protest brought back the pain in her legs and in her back that was always there in the background. Helen said "I'll have to sit-down" and she went back into the drawing-room. It looked as if she was running away, and Pat followed her.

Unwilling to believe that Helen, her best friend, could let her down, Pat began frantically to wave the bill at her and was almost shouting "Here! – Look at it! You must remember, Helen – when Tim promised he'd not expect anything from me if there was no Agent's Fee."

But Helen just sat there, with her mouth open and gasping, and gripping onto the arms of her chair. She looked up and saw Tim, her husband, whom she was beginning to loathe, and she saw Pat, her one, best, only friend. She knew that Pat was in the right, and that this was Tim's latest, cruellest trick. Oh, how she despised him! How she despised the mean, little man! But the terrible pain was there, now; bringing-back all the years when she'd hardly been able to walk and when she'd had to rely on Tim and daddy for everything; and then, later, on Tim alone, when daddy was gone. Even now she was helpless without Tim, and he knew it, and she hated him for the way he was exploiting it. Tim had made himself indispensable, and if, now, she thwarted Tim, she'd be alone and helpless. Nobody, not even Pat, could take Tim's place, and look after her.

Pat was getting desperate "Say something, Helen; please."

Tim broke-in "I approached Sykes-Waterhouse on your instructions, Pat. I was acting as your Agent. In my professional capacity I expect a Fee."

"Helen!" Pat said desperately "Helen – how can you let him do it?"

At last, Helen found a small voice, and, unable to meet Pat's eye, she whispered "He's my husband, Pat. A wife's first duty is to stand by her husband; don't you see?"

Pat shrieked, and ran out, into the drive, and drove away.

Helen stayed, sitting in the chair and sobbing quietly. Tim said "People have no right to presume on friendship. I'm the best surveyor in Liverpool. I'm well-respected – ask the manager at Sykes-Waterhouse. Pat Curry's had a full structural survey on her cottage; and professional representation with Estate Agents. She's like all the rest of your friends: she wants to get everything; and to pay nothing!"

"But, Tim" – Helen knew she had to speak, and she spoke with difficulty "Pat never approached you – none of my friends ever made the first approach. It was you who approached Pat. You persuaded her to have the survey; and it was you who asked her to let you share the Agent's Fee."

"Of course" he said, and there was triumph in his voice, as if, by her own words she'd clinched the argument for him "A professional man has a right to expect his friends to employ him."

She started to protest, but he interrupted "I expect your friends to give me their business, Helen. Let me make that clear, once and for all."

Helen said "I don't feel well, Tim. The pain in my legs: I've not felt as bad as this for years."

He helped her upstairs, and into the bedroom. She felt so helpless and her tone was humble when she said "I hope I'm not going to be a burden again, Tim."

He knew he'd won, and he could afford to be magnanimous. He almost smiled when he replied "You were never a burden, Helen. For me, it's been a privilege to look-after you."

He helped her to get into bed, and she felt humble, and passive, and gave him a grateful smile. But, underneath, she was hating him for what he'd done to Pat, and hating herself for having to depend on a mean, little man.

He said "I'll make supper. I'll bring a tray up for you."

She listened to him going downstairs, and the sound of his feet on the stairs wasn't the slow tread of a beaten man. He was in better spirits than he'd been for weeks, and she knew it was because her relapse made her even more dependent on him. She lay there, all tensed-up in bed, and the bedroom felt like a prison cell, with Tim as her gaoler. She hated him for her dependence on him, and for the way she'd had to be a traitor to her best and only friend.

Tim came upstairs with the tray and sat-down on the edge of the bed, to share the supper with her. He said "It's cosy, with just ourselves, together."

She said "That's what you've always wanted, Tim: just you and me – not even daddy. Just you, with me here in your power."

He said "You're depressed now, so you're saying things you don't mean."

She said "I wish you hadn't alienated all my friends, Tim."

He said "Everyone's against us, Helen. It's better that we face the truth."

She said "Not everyone, Tim."

He stood-up suddenly, and he had that look that frightened her, the half-mad staring look. He said "Everyone, Helen! – The Jews: Gerald Rinkman and all the Jews. As for Pat Curry and all your friends – they haven't the guts to face the Jews."

How she dreaded him going-on about Jews, and, to humour him, she said "As long as I've got you, Tim, I'll be well-protected from the Jews."

He was standing straight, now, at attention beside the bed. "Sieg Heil!" he shouted, and thrust his arm "Shall I wear my uniform tonight?"

She could see it was what he wanted, so she said "I'd like that, Tim." In a way, she wanted it, too; she knew that the man she had to depend on was a mean little man, but, somehow, she could stop despising herself for depending on him when he was in his Blackshirt uniform.

He stamped upstairs to the cupboard in the attic, and when he stamped downstairs again, he was in his hard, high boots. "Sieg Heil!" he snapped, and thrust his arm.

"Oh, Tim!" she said, and he was no longer the mean man she despised, but a jack-booted Nazi trampling everyone under his heel: trampling Gerald Rinkman who'd left her in pain; and trampling the Jews. She raised her arms up to him, like a suppliant, and he knew it was her old lust for the uniform again. "You're not well, Helen" he said "You mustn't strain yourself."

"I'm better now; truly Tim" she said; and she really did feel better, with the pain pushed into the background where it belonged. "I want you, Tim." she said.

"Sieg Heil!" he clicked his heels, and loosened his belt; and he looked-down proudly at where he was hard as steel, and she was staring at him. He said "The S.S. recruits were each given a dagger and a pet dog. To prove his loyalty the recruit had to stab the dog to death."

She said "That was cruel, Tim."

He said "Cruel, but necessary. Sometimes you have to take a dagger to a friend."

She whispered "You made me stab Pat in the back, Tim."

He did not deign to deny it, or to try to mask the cruelty in his voice. He said "My dagger's ready for you, Helen. Unsheathed, and hard as steel."

It excited Helen: the idea of a dagger and of a man so heartless he could stab his friend to death; a man with a black heart, dressed all in black, and with a dagger thrust-out at her like a Fascist salute.

"Sieg Heil!" she found herself screaming.

"Death to all Jew-lovers!" he shouted "Death to Pat Curry!" and, with that, he lunged. He lay over her and lunged; stabbing and stabbing; thrusting the hard steel, like an S.S.

dagger thrust deep into the heart of a German Shepherd dog. He seemed to hear the beating sound of drums, and the tramp of iron heels; and the roar of a million voices shouting for the Fuhrer, and against the Jews.

He made his final thrust; the coup-de-grace. And Helen felt the dagger twisting deeper. She said "You are so masterful, Tim." That's all that she wanted: for him to be dressed all in black and masterful, and not to be a mean, little man.

He said "You don't know how lucky you are, Helen. So many women are disappointed when they have sex. They get taken-in by men who are flashy on the tennis court, and flashy in their cars – and, afterwards they wonder why they're disappointed in bed."

"Jews are always trying to be flashy!" she sneered; she knew it was what he wanted to hear. But the memory had never left her of a hotel room that overlooked a lake, and a dark lover who was as masterful in bed as on the tennis court. She said "You're so masterful in your Blackshirt uniform, Tim."

He said "Pat Curry's a traitor Helen: as bad as Gerald Rinkman. The black uniform leaves no doubt about loyalties; it gives us the courage to stab, right to the heart."

Helen whispered "Pat's not like Gerald Rinkman, Tim. Pat's not a Jew."

"She's worse!" he shouted "She's a Jew-lover! She's worse than a Jew."

CHAPTER TWELVE

Colonel Gerald Rinkman, M.C. had returned as a hero from the war, but bitter, as only a Jew could be bitter. Right up to the end of the war, he'd thought he was inured and no longer shockable, after all that he'd seen: tanks in the North African desert all burnt-out, with human bodies inside like burnt-toast; and all the other abominations of war. But then he saw the Death-Camps, and his emotional armour proved to be even less effective than chain-mail against bullets. The horror was still with him, day and night, even in his sleep. As a Jew he felt exposed and vulnerable, even in England where now, after the war and the Holocaust, to be a Jew was to be everybody's friend.

For Gerald the mental image of those tortured Jewish bodies was inseparable from another image: of men stamping – marching and stamping – over their victims; of stamping, goose-stepping men dressed all in black. In Gerald's nightmares, the stamping, arrogant, cruel men in black were not all Hitler's S.S.: many of them were Mosley's Blackshirts; and their face – they all had the same face – was always the face of Tim Leston.

Gerald had caught a glimpse of Tim Leston, once or twice in the street; it was inevitable, in the business district of Liverpool. And, of course, he couldn't help seeing Tim, sitting at the window of his prestigious office where he knew he'd be noticed. Gerald learnt that Helen had made a remarkable recovery that was near-miraculous. He sometimes even found himself regretting leaving Helen, but not really: Helen's inheritance was never going to be enough to compensate for a lifetime of caring for a cripple. Besides, Gerald's father had always wanted him to marry a Jewess. He'd wanted Jewish grandchildren: kosher, circumcised. He looked forward to his grandsons' Bar-Mitzvahs and all the Jewish things.

Shortly after the war, Gerald's father called Gerald into his office. He said "I can understand that you're attracted to Goy women; I was like that myself. Compared with Jewish girls, they're easy: Jewish girls are the ones with strict morals."

Gerald did not bother to contradict him, but he was remembering the morals of so many Jewish girls during the war, when all they had to barter with was their bodies. His father went on "Play around with Gentile girls, but marry a Jewess."

So that's what Gerald did; and it wasn't a success. That's why he sometimes found himself wishing that he'd not been so quick to run away from Helen, and to leave her dying in a ditch. Just occasionally he caught sight of her, and it was true, her recovery was almost a miracle. She had a limp, but she didn't use a stick; and she was still pretty.

Gerald married his Jewess, then, as the years went by and his marriage grew cold, he started going with Gentile women again. Some of them were married women, and, once or twice Gerald was tempted to try it on again with Helen. What sweet revenge that would be: to stamp on the face of a Blackshirt in revenge for them stamping on the faces of Jews! He could so easily have contrived a meeting with Helen, as if it was by chance.

It wasn't only in his Jewish marriage that Gerald Rinkman was frustrated: he was frustrated in his work as a provincial Solicitor. The practice brought in a good income, but, somehow, after the intense years of the war, of being a hero and popular in the Officers' Mess, life was too mundane for Gerald. He'd been very young to be a Colonel, but he'd proved he could lead men in action. His life now was an anti-climax after all that.

At home too, it wasn't so much that he was sexually frustrated: his Gentile good-time girls took care of that. But the home his wife kept had become, somehow, alien; he'd felt far more at home in the Officers' Mess. This Jewish home of his in Liverpool, was homely all right, but it wasn't his type of home: it was his wife's type of home, a women's den: with all her women-friends, every one of them a Jewess, seemed to be always in the house; with a constant supply of cakes coming out of the kitchen, as if from a bakery. All the women were growing fat on the cakes, not least his wife: all of them not caring a damn about it, now that they were securely married, with Jewish husbands and families – that's what was important to them: a Jewish husband, and a good income, and security.

Gerald knew that there was no point in complaining, and, when he began to go out more and more often in the evenings his wife didn't seem to notice, or to care. Gerald became bored with good-time girls, so when the local Tory Party asked him to stand for the City Council he jumped at it. They said he'd have no trouble getting elected, being a war-hero and everything; even being a Jew was no longer a handicap, not like before the war. If anything it was an advantage, with everyone being so sorry about the way Jews had suffered.

The Tories were right, and Gerald was elected. Soon afterwards he became a member of the Council Planning Committee, so he got to know all about applications for permission to develop land for building. His Council work became more than just a hobby for him, and added spice to his bland working day. Even if he'd wished to do so, he'd have found it difficult to keep the two apart: his work as a lawyer and his Council Planning work. Planning became his hobby, and he was like a philatelist who pores over his stamp collection late into the night. Only, it wasn't old stamps that Gerald pored over, but old plans and documents.

Another commitment that Gerald became involved with was his work for Jewish charities. It wasn't exactly a hobby, but it was something important to him; something to sooth a mind haunted by images of death. It was a paradox that a man who'd been so callous that he'd left the girl he'd said he loved to die in a ditch, should now so unselfishly devote himself to a charity. But those images that haunted Gerald would have roused pity in anyone, except, perhaps, a Blackshirt.

The only charities Gerald would ever have considered were Jewish charities; he'd have given neither money nor commitment to a Christian charity. In a sense, Gerald did not work for the recipients of the Jewish charities, but for himself. He'd seen the tortured faces in the Concentration Camps, and in them he seemed to see a mirror-image of himself. In working to help the survivors of those Camps he was working to help himself. He could not bear to think of the victims being helped by Christian charity, thus putting all Jews, himself included, in debt to Christians. The only charity a Jew could accept without degradation, he believed, was charity from a fellow Jew. Gerald helped to raise money – there were Jewish agencies everywhere, raising money – and the money went towards providing Homes for the Jews who'd survived particularly for the few of them who were allowed to settle in England.

The City Council had documents: old maps and plans, and copies of title-deeds. Late one night, Gerald was poring over a bundle of documents, when there, before him, was a document as rare as a penny-black, and, to Gerald, infinitely more valuable. It was a document conveying title to a small strip of land. The Council had acquired the land many years ago for a proposed new road, but the scheme had been dropped, and the land forgotten, because it was adjacent to a public park. The exciting thing for Gerald, that made the document more valuable to him than a penny-black, was that, whereas the park was open land for all time, the strip of land was not.

Together with the document was an old map of the

area, and it seemed familiar to Gerald. Yes, he recognised the area; he'd often driven around it before the war. How could he ever forget when the car he'd been driving had been as feline as the girl who'd been sitting beside him?

He studied the map – yes, it was the same place, and he remembered vividly, as if he'd only been there yesterday, the view from the back of Helen's father's house, across the garden to the wall and the park beyond. Without the map and the document nobody would have guessed that the strip of undergrowth immediately behind the wall was separate from the park.

As he sat there, concentrating on the map, he began to think of Helen, and how pretty she had been. And he thought of Tim Leston who'd be there, now, with Helen in the house: Tim Leston, the Blackshirt who had, at their last confrontation, spat-out Gerald's name in the way that Antonio had spat on Shylock. He thought of Tim Leston the Blackshirt, and of the black-uniformed, black-hearted S.S. guards at the Camps, and he thought of a million goose-stepping boots stamping on the faces of Jews. He thought of these things, and, more than anything in the world, he wanted to hit back; he wanted his revenge – the revenge of all Jews – on those Camp guards and on Tim Leston the Blackshirt. He wanted to gather together all those poor Jews, those victims of the Holocaust, those mirror-images of himself, and to establish them there, on that strip of land; so that they would be always there, above the wall, looking down on the Blackshirt. So that Tim Leston, the Blackshirt, could never, ever, forget, that the Jews were superior to him, and looking down.

He thought of Helen too, and of the hurt she'd suffer: for the second time he'd make her suffer. But why should he hesitate over one Gentile girl when there had been so many thousands of Jews? Starved to death, broken and twisted, and thrown down, all heaped together, into mass-graves? And thousands, thousands more – millions – driven by blackshirted guards into gas-chambers, and burnt-up in a great, anonymous Holocaust?

Gerald didn't act in person – he was too canny for that. He acted through one of the Jewish charities, impersonally. On their behalf, he offered the City Council an attractive price for the strip of land as building land. The Planning application had to come before the Planning Committee of the City Council of course, and then it had to be ratified by the whole Council: a mere formality. But first, like all Planning applications, it had to be published in the Press, and neighbours given an opportunity to object. Of course, Gerald should have declared an interest and abstained from the discussion and the vote, and that's what eventually provoked Tim Leston into Libel. But Gerald Rinkman was too shrewd a lawyer to lay himself open, and he hid his interest behind a legal technicality.

Tim's objections came before the Planning Committee, as Gerald Rinkman knew they would; he'd have been disappointed if the Blackshirt had surrendered without a fight. The Jew in Gerald wanted to humiliate the Blackshirt, and the lawyer in him wanted to humiliate the upstart surveyor. Tim made a very strong case, and Gerald reluctantly had to admit that to himself. Only a surveyor like Tim could have made so much out of the ancient Covenants, and only a lawyer like Gerald could have found a way around the Covenants, to confound Tim with the law. He argued that the Covenants were not enforceable, because of the lapse of time, and because of the changed ownership of the properties. The matter went to court.

Instead of instructing a lawyer, Tim presented affidavit evidence himself. He wanted to berate Gerald Rinkman as a scheming Jew, who was misusing his position on the Council, and to urge the Judge to enforce the Covenants, rather than betray England to the Jews. Unfortunately for Tim, the

150

procedure of the Court gave him no opportunity. The judgement was that the Covenants were not enforceable, which left the Council free to sell the land as building land.

Gerald left the Court in triumph. Once more he felt he was doing something vital, and winning, in a way he'd not felt since he'd won his M.C. in the war. He'd grown a moustache during the war, an officer's moustache, and, as he left the Court, he gave his moustache a little twist of victory. The sale of the land to the Jewish charity was completed almost immediately, and the sense of post-war anti-climax, which, for Gerald, had almost become a depression, lifted at last.

Gerald often visited the building-site, and every brick that was laid was like a brick thrown in defiance against the Fascists and the Nazis; and later, when the building was completed, every Jewish refugee who was offered shelter meant one less tortured body to haunt Gerald Rinkman in his dreams.

What Tim Leston did next was so preposterous that not even Gerald Rinkman could have expected it. Just as Antonio had done with Shylock, so did Tim Leston the Blackshirt put himself at the mercy of Gerald Rinkman the Jew.

When the Chairman of the City Council – the Mayor – showed Gerald the letter he'd received from Tim, Gerald knew he had Tim at this mercy. Right away his mind began to revolve like a whetting-stone and to hone a cutting Libel-case for Court.

The actual Libel case was a disappointment for Gerald. Oh! it had been satisfaction to anticipate the High-Court hearing and the prospect of his victim twitching on the blade; but when, instead, the Blackshirt poured-out his anti-Semitic bile, and the Judge did little to stop him, it was the victims of the Holocaust who screamed-out for mercy, in Gerald's mind, instead of the hated Blackshirt who should have been screaming under the knife.

It took all of Gerald's capacity for self-control to resist the temptation to rant-back at Tim in court: to denounce him as a Nazi and a Fascist, and to make the mistake of appealing to the Jury as if they, too, were Jews. He looked at the Judge, and he looked at the Jury, and he was overtaken by a terrible illusion that they were all wearing black shirts, and that the faces of the Jurymen and women were the death's-head faces of the S.S. Guards in the Camps.

He wanted to cry-out; to stand and shout. But he forced himself to stay seated, and to listen to everything that Tim said. He forced himself to be the Professional Lawyer: Plaintiff and Plaintiff's Counsel, all at once.

The Jury found for Gerald Rinkman the plaintiff – it was a foregone conclusion. But the damages were derisory. It was an insult as hard to bear as the spittle Shylock had had to take from Antonio. Like Shylock, Gerald Rinkman had to smile a sickly smile; but, unlike the time before, when he'd left the other Court with a twirl of his moustache, this time, when he left, he felt that everyone was mocking him; as though they were all pointing a finger at the Jew – as though, he, Gerald Rinkman, was wearing a Yellow Star. In his mind he could hear the sound of shattering glass, and the glass was that of the Jewish shopfronts on crystal-night. He felt hunted, and he wanted to run, and his only consolation was that even if the damages were derisory, the costs would be anything but derisory, and Tim must be getting very short of funds.

Time passed, and Gerald's post-war depression, that had been dispelled for a while, returned. People forgot that Gerald Rinkman had been a war-hero, and the Jewish family-life that his wife made for him seemed less and less relevant to Gerald who, really, had no wish for a Jewish identity. Gerald had been happiest when he'd been amongst his Gentile fellow-officers in the Mess; he'd been eager to join a Gentile tennis club; and he'd been so keen on a Gentile girl that he'd stolen her from his friend.

Time passed slowly for Gerald, as the grey time always does, and Gerald's keen mind grew blunt from the kind of work he had to do; provincial lawyers' work, concerned mostly with property: conveyancing, and Wills and the like.

As soon as she moved into her new cottage, Pat Curry became all bubbly again. It would have taken more than Tim Leston to burst the bubbles for ever. Pat was determined that whatever Tim had done, it wouldn't end her friendship with Helen, and she couldn't count how often she'd lifted the telephone to ring her; but she always replaced it, in case it was Tim who answered. She was afraid of what Tim would say to her, and what she'd say to Tim. The trouble was that Helen, because of her disabilities, could not drive a car; that was still the big threat Tim held over her: she depended on him for everything, especially for transport. Sometimes Pat thought that Helen rather liked to be so dependent on Tim, and used it as an excuse. After all, she could have called a taxi; she had only to lift the telephone to call a taxi, while Tim was at work, but she never did.

Pat had other girlfriends; she'd always had so many girlfriends, and, now that they were all married, she was auntie to all their children. So, because Helen never telephoned, or came to visit in a taxi, the friendship between Pat and Helen withered away.

CHAPTER THIRTEEN

It must have been two years since Pat had moved into her cottage, and she hadn't thought about Helen for ages, when something happened that certainly made her think of Helen, and of Tim, too; particularly Tim.

There was a cupboard in the small bedroom at the back of the house; Pat seldom opened the door of that bedroom, let alone the cupboard. She'd no need to go into the room, living on her own as she did. There were other, larger, spare bedrooms for visitors, and Pat had never felt she wanted to have anyone to share the house with her; she'd had enough of that, after all the years looking-after her mother. It was always a delicious feeling for Pat, to close the front-door against the world, and to do whatever she wanted; just to pamper herself, without anyone else to spoil it.

She often had friends to stay, but never for more than a few days; and she always put them in the bedroom next to her own bedroom at the front. So, there never seemed to be any need to use the bedroom at the back, or to open the cupboard which had been built-in around the chimney-breast.

There was a thunderstorm that night and a branch was split and swinging, and the garden was full of puddles. Pat couldn't think when she'd last needed wellies; she couldn't even remember where she'd put them at the time of her house-move.

The creaking of the broken branch began to get on Pat's nerves, and she knew she'd have to lop it, if she wanted any sleep. So she rummaged about for her wellies, all over the house.

It was when she opened the door of the cupboard that she saw the thing that shocked her into remembering Helen, and, particularly Tim. There was a gash in the wall, behind the cupboard door, like a gash of forked-lightning; and, when Pat opened the door, the wind and rain blew-in, through the gash,

154

and the night-sky flashed behind it. A bolt of thunder banged suddenly overhead, and the house trembled; while Pat stood mesmerised, staring at the gash and trembling as much as the house.

She stared for a long time, until the rumbles and the flashes moved away. Then, like an old soldier shrugging off defeat, the house moved, and the gash became a wide wound.

Pat shut the cupboard door, like someone unfamiliar with wounds trying to hide war's horrors under a blanket. She knew what she had to do; she had to call-in an expert, and do it quickly. The expert she knew she must call-in was the only one who really knew the house; the expert who'd carried-out the full structural survey two years before, and who'd passed the house as fit, in the way an Army doctor passes men as being fit for battle. She knew she should telephone for Tim Leston, but she couldn't bring herself to do it. She was already beginning to suspect that Tim had not only cheated her over his fee, but, even worse, had skimped his survey, thus putting at risk her precious house, like a quack doctor charging a fat fee for a false diagnosis.

There was a jobbing builder whose yard was up the road in Woolton village. His workshop had originally been a cottage in the old part of the village. There was a handcart in the yard, and a trailer full of bricks and rubble, and a battered van. Instead of telephoning Tim, Pat asked the builder to come and look at the crack, which even by daylight, looked as cruel as forked-lightning and as ominous as thunder.

The builder said "I can do the job; it will be a big job, but I can do it."

"A big job?" Pat asked in alarm.

The builder sensed the panic in her voice, and tried to reassure her "Best get a surveyor's report" he said "It may not be as bad as I think."

"What do you really think?" she said "I want to know

the truth. Please!"

He said "It might only be subsidence, though that would be bad enough. But I'm afraid it could be even worse. These old cottages – they're pretty; but they don't last for ever."

She interrupted him. "What if it's only subsidence?" she said.

He measured his words. He didn't want to upset her, but he wouldn't give her false hope "If it's only subsidence, we can dig-out the footings; strengthen the foundations. – You should be able to get your Insurance Company to pay for subsidence."

He paused for his words to sink in "I'd be happier if you got a surveyor's report before I started."

She said "I had a full structural survey, before I moved in."

"Did the surveyor not warn you about the wall?" he said.

"No" she answered "No. He found no serious faults. He said the house was sound."

"Well then!" the builder said, and he was smiling now – he'd no need to worry about upsetting her now; here was a let-out, and no mistake. "You've no need to worry" he said "Surveyors are covered by their own Indemnity Insurance. Your Surveyor's Insurance Company will pay."

She felt the pressure on her lift, in the way that atmospheric pressure lifts after thunder passes; the sky was bright again, and the birds were singing.

The builder was saying "You'll have to approach your surveyor; the one that did the structural survey. I'll be able to follow his report, and then give you an estimate for the job."

There was just the one small cloud: the thought of approaching Tim Leston. But, when Pat did telephone, he was all charm; he said he was so glad to hear from her, and, if there was a problem, he'd come round right away. He was with her within the hour, in his car, and Pat wondered whether he was getting much business, if he had so much time to spare and at such short notice.

He came in all smiles, and saying "Pat! – Helen keeps asking why you never come to visit."

She showed him the gash in the wall, which was like a tree split by a thunderbolt, and he was full of concern. He took measurements, and followed the thunderbolt-split down, through the house, where it went to earth behind the roses.

Pat said "The builder told me you'd be insured, Tim."

Tim smiled his thin smile and kept on talking in his over-confident Blackshirt way. But he didn't feel confident; it was more like panic that he was feeling. He said "I'll send you a full report in the post."

He wanted time to think.

At home, he said nothing to Helen. He just went to the room which had been Helen's father's study, but which Tim now used as an office. He closed the door behind him, and took-out his copy of the Structural Survey. He already knew it was a worthless survey: skimped; the only bit of worthless, skimped work he'd ever done. It had been his way of paying-back what he'd taken to be an insult: that someone who claimed to be Helen's friend should question his right to charge a fee. How ironic, he thought bitterly, if Tim Leston, the master-Surveyor, whose work was always so thorough it was a byword amongst builders and Estate Agents – a byword especially at Sykes-Waterhouse. – How ironic, if Tim Leston should be found negligent. The disgrace would be unbearable!

How ironic if the master-surveyor, whose work was always so meticulous that almost alone amongst surveyors he had no need of Professional Indemnity Insurance – for why should a master-surveyor subsidise the blunders of lesser, fallible men? – How ironic if he, the great surveyor, should be destroyed, like Lucifer, through over-confidence and pride!

Tim laughed; a mirthless, manic laugh. Helen heard

him, from the other end of the house, and it frightened her.

Tim thought hard; then, carefully, he wrote his report, and his covering letter to Pat. The report was accurate, and thorough as only the report of a master-surveyor could be. He described the necessary building work: the strengthening of the foundations, and the rebuilding of part of the wall. But the covering letter was not the work of a master-surveyor; it was the work of a master-deceiver as black as Lucifer. In his opinion, Tim wrote, the structural problems were of very recent origin, and his original survey was not at fault.

Then – and he laughed again, like Lucifer – he typed-out his bill: his account-rendered for his site visit, for his advice on structural repairs, and for his Surveyor's Report.

The envelope came through Pat's letter-box the next morning. At first it was only the Report that she read. She had to sit-down, holding the report, feeling as fearful for her cottage as a mother for a sick child. Then she read the covering letter, and her mind began to race madly, between tears and anger. She looked-out across the garden, and, although the weather was fine, the day seemed oppressive, and charged with thunder.

It was spoiled, all spoiled; with her pretty cottage split apart by forked lightning. She felt like giving-in. How could she hope to defeat a man who had the power to strike her with lightning, like Lucifer? Or with a thunderbolt, like Thor?

Tim Leston was a Blackshirt bully, and he frightened her. She felt she'd have to give-in, for the sake of peace; she'd have to give-in. After all, it was a Master-Surveyor of the Chartered Institute who had submitted this report! Listlessly she turned the envelope, and another slip of paper fell-out. It was the bill: the account rendered! – Not only had Tim Leston cheated her, he was even making her pay for it!

She stood-up and screamed; but, when the long scream ended, Pat Curry was no longer close to tears. She was as desperate as a female animal who turns, at last, at bay, to fight the snapping predator. For the first time in her life Pat Curry was ready to stand-up against a man, and the precious thing which drove her to fight was the life of the cottage she loved.

She thought of Helen, and she was surprised how unemotional she felt about her. She remembered how, before her accident, all the men used to buzz-about Helen, and how she, Pat, had stayed in the background behind the teacups. That made her think of Gerald Rinkman and how all the girls wanted him to notice them, and how she, Pat, had wanted it so much that she ached. But, of course, the only girl that Gerald Rinkman did notice was the girl all the men always noticed: Helen Pringle. She remembered Gerald's car, and how feline it was and the way it purred; and how Helen Pringle purred too, like a cat that knows it's the centre of attention.

And she remembered Tim Leston: Tim, who'd been Helen's little mouse; Helen's own, pet mouse that she played with, and held, trapped, between her paws. And how the little mouse was, suddenly, spurned, and so became as vicious as one of those black rats that carry the plague.

She remembered the time when she heard about Helen's accident, and how terrible it was; and how pitiful Helen looked when she visited her in hospital: like a pet that has been run-over and thrown into a ditch.

After the accident it was Helen who needed Pat, and it was a thrill for Pat that Helen took so much notice of her. So, for years, Pat was Helen's best friend; the only friend who refused to be driven-away by Tim.

At first everyone had marvelled at Tim, and the way he went back to Helen after she'd been ditched by Gerald. But Tim became so strange! It was so strange that a man who'd been the tennis club mouse – less significant even than a rabbit – should now have become as vicious as a black rat carrying the plague. It was the Black Death that Tim Leston carried, and some people said they'd seen him in his black-shirted Black Death uniform, sidling like a rat, close to the wall, on his way to Lime Street Station, to catch the London train.

Pat remembered those old newspapers, and the reports of the Blackshirt Rallies; and Sir Oswald Mosley's warnings against the enemy within. Once there had been a picture in the paper of Tim Leston in the front rank of the Blackshirts with his arm thrust forward and looking as vicious as the plague.

Then there was that terrible night at the tennis club, and Tim Leston the Blackshirt, insulting Gerald Rinkman the Jew. The night when so many of the other men in the club shamefully showed their colours: that their hearts were as black as Tim Leston's black shirt. The black rat-pack had turned against the Jew, and had driven him out.

It had been terrible for Pat who had watched it all from her place behind the teacups. At the time she hadn't been able to decide who was worse: the cruel Blackshirt or the heartless Jew. How could Gerald Rinkman have been so heartless as to ditch Helen like that? Like a dog that he'd run over, and thrown into a ditch? – He was so heartless, and yet so attractive! If only he'd been aware of the hopeless heartache of the girl behind the teacups, and how she'd romanticised about him and his car: how, in her dreams, the girl sitting beside Gerald in the car was not Helen Pringle, but Pat Curry – rescued from behind the teacups by the charming Prince Gerald himself.

For a long while Pat sat there, remembering everything and holding Tim's bill and report in her hand. She knew, of course, all about Tim's long battle with Gerald. She'd heard it all from Helen; how Gerald had viciously taken his pound of flesh. Pat had sympathised with Helen, as a best girl-friend ought to sympathise, and she'd shared Helen's hatred of the Jew.

But, what now? Pat's thoughts were no longer

sympathetic but cold. One thing was clear: in all that long-running battle of hatred and revenge, Gerald Rinkman had always been the winner. The war-hero knew how to fight, and how to take advantage over his enemy. Gerald Rinkman's enemy was now Pat's own enemy too, and so, Gerald Rinkman would be her best ally.

She looked-up Gerald's business number in the telephone book and asked to speak to Mr. Rinkman personally. She said "Hello Gerald – this is Pat Curry. You won't remember me, but we were in the same tennis club." She spoke diffidently; she had never got over her shyness with men. She forced a laugh "I was the girl who always served the teas."

A vague memory came to Gerald of a shy girl he'd not had time to notice. "How nice!" he said "How nice to hear from you, Pat." He sounded charming; it was second nature to Gerald to sound charming. "Well, what can I do for you?" he said.

She explained about the crack in the wall that was like forked-lightning , and about the surveyor who refused to accept liability.

Gerald was only half listening. It was just another routine provincial-lawyer's case. He said "Don't worry, Pat. One of my junior partners will sort it out for you." He'd remembered her more clearly now: a girl who'd been as bland and as sweet as her own cream teas.

Pat sensed his indifference, and played her trump. "The Surveyor" she said "Was Tim Leston – I want you to take him on, and win."

Gerald tried to suppress his excitement. "You flatter me" he said "Come and see me in my office – tomorrow, ten o'clock."

Pat was punctual. Gerald's secretary showed her into Gerald's private office, and Gerald stood-up to greet her. She still felt shy, but she managed to smile and to shake his hand.

He was charming still, and still glamorous, with steel-grey strands in his black hair, and the same athletic frame he'd had on the tennis court.

She saw that he was appraising her, and she knew that he'd never have bothered about a sugar-and-cream girl in the old days. She's really quite attractive, he was thinking, and he found himself wondering if he'd developed a late taste for English clotted cream.

She said "I have the papers with me – Tim Leston did a structural survey two years ago; here it is. It makes no mention of serious faults, and now terrible cracks have appeared in a wall. Tim says that any faults are recent, and denies liability. But the local builder says the fault must have been there for years."

Gerald said "We'll get an independent surveyor's report – but Tim Leston's just being awkward. His Professional Indemnity Insurance will cover him."

Pat said "That's just what I told him myself, but he ignored me. Do you know – I don't believe he has any Insurance."

Gerald laughed "Now, wait a minute! No surveyor would be such a fool – certainly no surveyor who's a real professional. Whatever his faults, Tim Leston is a damned good surveyor, though I hate to admit it. He's proud of being professional."

"Oh!" said Pat, weakly "Well if that's the case, and you press him for payment, I'm sure his Insurance will pay."

But Gerald's mind was racing – What if she's right? – No; impossible! – Tim Leston would never expose himself to such a terrible risk! He'd never put himself at the mercy of an enemy, like Antonio did with Shylock! – Surely not? Why on earth would he do such a foolish thing?

But then, Gerald thought – perhaps, like Antonio, Tim Leston is short of money; and he's proud, just like Antonio: so proud he'd risk anything, his life even, to keep a proud face to the world. Like Antonio, Tim Leston had always been over-confident, and so certain of his place at the top of his profession that he might – he just might – have convinced himself that he was above such paltry considerations as Insurance, unlike lesser men.

That must be it! – Somehow, against all reason, Gerald knew he was right. He smiled a tight-lipped smile, like Shylock, and said "I know a good surveyor; one I can trust. I'll bring him around with me, to your house, tomorrow."

Gerald's surveyor friend was Jewish, and he worked for the same firm of Jewish architects who had designed the Home for Jewish Refugees, behind the Lestons' house. The Jewish surveyor knew all about Tim Leston; he hated Tim for being anti-Semitic, and he was jealous, too, of Tim being another surveyor who was good at his job.

As soon as the Jewish surveyor saw the lightning-crack in the wall he knew that it was the crack of doom for Tim. He had to force himself to give his opinion dispassionately, and unemotionally, but he couldn't disguise the triumph in his tone. He said "This wall has been dangerous for years." And, right away, he wrote-out, in his report, details of the necessary building works.

Pat asked him what it would all cost, and the surveyor advised her to get her builder to submit an estimate. "It won't be cheap" he said.

The surveyor left, and Gerald said "Would you like me to arrange it all for you, Pat?" He was smiling at her, and thinking that he'd like to taste English clotted-cream.

Pat felt flattered and warmed by his smile. He'd never smiled at her like that in the old days, at the tennis club. "I know I can trust you, Gerald" she said.

Gerald said "If only I'd been as perceptive when I was young as I am now! I'd never have made such a fool of myself over Helen Pringle."

Pat said "Helen Pringle – Helen Leston – was my best friend."

"Tim Leston was my best friend" Gerald said "Until he became my enemy, and the enemy of all Jews. Helen took advantage of your friendship, Pat, while Tim cheated you and jeopardised your house... Tim and Helen: two false friends, who deserve each other."

Pat said "Helen Pringle was so much fun, and so pretty. I'm not surprised you fell for her, Gerald."

Gerald said "You were pretty, too, Pat. You still are – but I was too taken-up with Helen to notice."

Pat blushed, and said "You'll stay for tea, Gerald?" and Gerald said "I should have taken more notice of the girl who served the teas."

Pat went into the kitchen to brew-up and Gerald followed her. The view was across the garden to a pond with a weeping-willow. How different from Gerald's own house, not far away, above Gateacre Brow in Childwall, which was all chrome, and glitzy, with its deep-pile carpet wall-to-wall, and its cocktail-bar. Gerald's wife would be there, now, at home, with her usual coterie of women-friends; like the Queen of Sheba holding court, all dark and matriarchal. They were handsome women, most of them, but overdressed. Lots of men – lots of Gentile men, even – would have found more at Gerald's house to whet their appetite, and more of the exotic, than here, in this cottage, with this faded English rose.

Gerald had to smile at himself for finding more of the exotic in a wilting rose than in the strongly-hued flowers of the Levant.

Pat was on the point of lifting the tea-tray. "Allow me!" Gerald said, and took it from her.

Pat served the tea, and that evoked memories. She said "The very first time you came to the club... you were so different from the other men."

"You mean – I was Jewish." he said.

"I mean you were a gentleman, and you had style" she replied. She was thinking about his stylish clothes, and stylish car; and about the stylish way he moved about the tennis-court.

He said "There were so many false friends. I was looking everywhere for true friends, Pat. If only I'd seen what was there all the time, behind the teacups!"

Pat said "You only had eyes for Helen Pringle."

"They were false friends" he said "Helen and Tim."

"I think Tim's mad" Pat said "I've heard him making excuses for the Nazis and for Auschwitz. He'd like to have seen the end of all Jews."

"Tim Leston would have liked to see me in Auschwitz" Gerald said "He'd willingly have locked the chamber door himself, and turned-on the gas." He paused, staring at the floor; remembering. At last he said "That's why I've got to defeat Tim Leston, Pat. We're in this together, now, you and I, and we've got to win."

She poured the tea, and offered Gerald a biscuit "I'm afraid they're not kosher" she said.

He laughed "It means nothing to me. I get so much of that kosher rammed down my throat at home, I could choke."

She said "So you're not really a Jew?"

He replied angrily "I'm a modern Jew. I follow Ben-Gurion, not Moses." He was leaning forward on his chair, and speaking fast "Oh yes, I'm a Jew. My father and mother were both Jews, and, for their sake, I married a Jewess. I had my Bar-Mitzvah and I'm circumcised. You want to see?" He was being brutal, now, and wanting to shock.

Pat caught her breath, and blushed, and looked away; sitting there, with her knees together, and her skirt pulled-down tight, and her heart hammering; and not daring to face him after the crude, violent, vehement things he was saying.

"You're an English girl; an English rose" he went on "Have you never seen a man who's circumcised?"

She was shocked, and she knew she must show him how shocked she was. But she was fascinated, too, and ashamed of herself for being fascinated. And frightened that, if she complained, he'd leave. She wanted to run out of the room, and tried to stand up, but he was holding her. She had a sensation of fear, but, at the same time, a sort of fascination, in the way that the Sabine women must have felt when they were raped. She managed to whisper "Please, Gerald! Try to calm yourself."

But he was as insistent and hot as only a man of the Levant can be. "Have you never seen a man who's circumcised?" he repeated.

"I can't believe you're really saying these things" she said; and then, because he kept on holding her, and insisting on a reply, she whispered desperately "I've never seen any man in that way... in the way you're meaning."

It was not a possibility that he'd even contemplated – she must be nearly forty, now. "You're still a virgin?" he said; and, when she nodded, he added "I'm sorry Pat. I'm sorry if I've insulted you."

She watched him; watched him as he changed from being a terrible Levantine, intent on rape, back into being a respectable lawyer: an English gentleman, despite his Jewishness. The crisis was over, and she should have felt relief, but what, to her own amazement, she actually felt was anticlimax, and disappointment. She felt as disappointed as if she'd been the only wallflower who'd not been deflowered, amongst all the Sabine women. She'd read so much in women's magazines about the joys of climax, and now this anticlimax made her desperate. She found herself screaming at him "Show me! Show me! – You said you'd show me where you're circumcised!"

Her cry was as sharp as the thorn of the rose; and she was wild as the wild-rose, like an English tea-rose that's reverted to the briar-wild. She was on him, and over him, with all the pent-up frustration of so many years released at last. She was clutching at him, clumsily and tight around him, there, where he was hard as a thorn; and her nails were sharp as thorns where they pressed. His Levant blood was roused, and, once again, he shed the thin skin of an English gentleman as easily as he'd lost his infant-skin when it had been cut by the Rabbi.

"Look then!" he cried "Look!" as he unzipped and thrust-out. "There" he shouted, and held her hand hard on him "Now you know I'm a Jew! – There, where the fruit was peeled by the Rabbi's knife."

Pat held tight; it was a compulsion to hold tight. And she stared-down, as tense and as rigid as the object of her stare. She felt the warm dampness inside herself, where she was moist and aching for him: aching for the peeled fruit; for the forbidden fruit; for the fruit of the tree of knowledge. She did not bother to feign reluctance and to play the part of Pat Curry, the girl behind the teacups, who everyone always assumed was somebody else's girl. She said "I don't want to stay a virgin all my life."

If only he knew what it had taken for her to say it! It was a metamorphosis as absolute as that of Lamia who shed her snake's skin, to reveal herself a woman; as absolute as that of an infant boy whose skin is cut by a Rabbi to reveal the Jew inside.

"Where shall we go?" he asked.

"The room with the crack" she replied "It will be our secret room."

"That's fitting" he said "It will be the English Rose and the Star of David, united against the Swastika and the lightning-flash."

The room was full of old-fashioned things that Pat had brought from her mother's house. Things she didn't really want, like the old bed in which her mother had died. It was an old-fashioned bed, and it creaked when Pat lay-down across it. She felt all flushed and rumpled, in her inexperience; still wearing her knickers and with her skirt riding-up in creases, up to her hips.

She hadn't bothered to close the cupboard door after the surveyor's inspection, and the door hung open, showing the cruel gash in the wall.

Gerald spoke apologetically "I'll have to undress" he said and Pat watched him as he took-off his suit, and tie, and shoes and socks.

She did nothing; and he said "You'll have to undress, too." But all she did was pull-off her knickers, before lying-back again, and staring; staring up at him, at where he was circumcised.

He sensed that she was having doubts, and he said "Look – you don't have to carry on, if you don't want." His tone was half-apologetic, and she might have taken the escape-route he offered; but, suddenly, she had a vision of the years ahead and of the unknown fruit of the tree, and of eternal anticlimax. She said "Have you forgotten about the Rose and the Star against the Swastika?" and she pointed to the gash in the wall. It maddened her to see the gash and to remember the complacent look on Tim Leston's face when he'd tried to justify his fee. She almost sneered when she said "Have you forgotten that Tim Leston would not hesitate to lock the chamber door and to turn-on the gas?"

She was mocking him, and it maddened him. He said "I'll show you that Jews can fight back. Thank God for modern Israel!"

She continued to mock; she was finding it exciting to provoke him. "Did I hear you say Thank God? – You follow

168

Ben-Gurion, remember, not Moses."

He looked down at her, where she was waiting for him: all flushed and frightened, and determined, all at once. He said "If you're really sure, Pat."

She looked up at him and her fear, now, was that he really didn't want her, and that all this concern for her feelings was just a show. She said "Perhaps it's you that's having second thoughts?"

He looked down at her, and, yes, she was a windblown Rose, and past her best; but still, she was an English tea-Rose, and his thorn was hard. He said "I do want you, Pat; truly. The Rose and the Star, united against the Swastika!"

With clumsy instinct, she reached-down to part herself, where her hair was soft as a dandelion-clock. Still he stood there, above her, and he was hard as the Staff of Moses when Moses struck the rock. He looked down at where she had parted herself, and his thoughts were of summer days, and of English hedgerows and wild flowers. She's so unlike our Jewish girls, he was thinking – Their hair is dark, there, and they are as hot as the sun. He thought of the Staff of Moses striking the rock, and of the cool spring that gushed. Then he thought of the burning bush: two thoughts inspired by Moses – the cool spring and the fiery bush. He'd always yearned for a cool English spring, and he'd never really wanted a burning Levantine bush. He'd only agreed for the sake of his father: to Bar-Mitzvah, and to marriage with a Jewish girl; and so to immolation inside a burning bush. All he had to do, now, was to strike the rock with his own Staff and the cool, cool, spring would gush-forth, and douse the fire; and quench his thirst in a cool, English stream.

He said "I don't want to hurt you, Pat." But she didn't care. She said "I'm too old to worry about that. I haven't time to worry, Gerald."

He came into her, and he was hard, and, really, she was

not too tight. There was a little pain, but she didn't care. Her skirt was in creases, up round her waist, and there was a warm dampness, and no longer a cool stream: little beads of dampness on her face, and the damp warmth coming up from deep within her, where he'd struck her with his Staff.

Gerald smiled – how could he have imagined that the spring would stay cool? It was a hot spring after all, as hot as any spring in Israel; but still, it was a stream capable of dousing a burning bush.

She felt how proud he was, and it was wonderful to feel him proud, with his staff, and its point that was never sheathed. She said "It's wonderful, Gerald. I've had to wait so long for this."

He thrust, hard, just once to make her feel him, and to feel the unsheathed point. The pain had gone, for Pat, and it was wonderful to feel him.

"More!" she said "Again, please!"

He said "You make me feel strong; I was a fool not to notice the Rose behind the teacups."

She was wild now, as wild as a bramble-rose, and it was wonderful. She wanted him to thrust, and thrust again, and to strike with his staff. She shouted "More, Gerald. More, please!", and when he struck, and struck again she felt herself wanting to call-out. "Look, everyone! – Can't you see? It's Gerald Rinkman, the most attractive man in the Club. And the girl he's with isn't Helen Pringle; it's Pat Curry."

He was moving fast now, and striking faster. It was unstoppable, now that he was striking fast and deep. The deep, deep waters of the spring were rising; rising and rising from the secret depths of the rock; and rising, gushing, like a glorious fountain, gushing up towards the sun.

Gerald was shouting something, and in that glorious moment, when the water from the spring exploded – when, for the first time in her life, Pat felt the spring exploding within her towards the sun – Pat thought she heard what he was shouting, and it was "Victory!"

He was panting, now, and his staff was limp. He said "You might get pregnant... I never thought...."

"I don't care" she said.

He came out of her, and she lay there; happy and not caring: a woman, at last.

He said "I hope this won't be the only time; my English Rose!"

She said "You're welcome, Gerald. Welcome any time."

He said "We'll be meeting for business quite often, until we get this thing with Tim Leston settled. There's no reason why we shouldn't meet for business here." He dressed, and took his leave, but Pat didn't move. She just stayed, lying on the bed, and staring at the crack in the wall.

CHAPTER FOURTEEN

The Jewish surveyor's detailed written report came promptly, and it was damning. The fault in the wall must have been obvious for at least five years' he wrote. The foundations of the house needed to be reinforced, and the wall partly rebuilt.

Gerald arranged a site-meeting with the local builder, and the surveyor; and the provisional estimate for the building work was so high that Pat was shocked.

The builder and the surveyor left. Gerald could see that Pat was angry: like a Rose that was all thorns and ready to scratch. He said "If Tim Leston won't pay up, we'll take him to Court. We'll get our pound of flesh."

"I want more than a pound of flesh" she said "I want his heart."

Gerald said "When you said that you guessed that Tim wasn't insured, I scoffed. But, now, I think you may be right... If he really is not insured, you'll get his heart and more. Helen will have to sell her house. That would tear-out Helen's heart as well as Tim's."

She said "Helen was my best friend. But why should Helen keep her house intact, while Tim gets away with tearing the heart out of mine?"

It was making Gerald wild, to watch this faded Rose revitalised by hate. He'd had plenty of young women: pretty women who were all very English; he could take his pick of the Roses he chose to pluck. His wife must have suspected, but she didn't seem to care, so long as she could hold her own court at home, like Sheba. And yet, there was something different – something obsessive and incestuous even, in this hot desire of his for a faded woman revitalised by hate: Pat and Gerald were bound together in a union as strong as blood, by their mutual hatred of the Blackshirt.

These thoughts raced incoherently through Gerald's

mind, and his lust for Pat was as strong as blood-lust. She'd been the anaemic girl behind the teacups, but now she'd drunk the red-hot blood of hate. She said "That room, – our room Gerald. It will be our room for as long as the crack stays in the wall."

He followed her upstairs, and this time she wasn't shy. Ever since the first time, she'd been anticipating more: wanting and waiting; searching her own body, and wondering why she'd never searched before. She thought of all those years behind the teacups, and searched herself like a wanton; and the mere memory of the hard staff that had struck the rock, was enough to tap the spring.

That first time, she'd been too shy to undress, and had allowed her skirt to ride-up, rumpled. But now he watched her as, deliberately she removed her clothes, and stood before him, naked. "You too, Gerald" she said.

He undressed, and they stood there, a little apart. It was incomprehensible to Gerald that he should feel such hot lust for a woman he'd hardly noticed when she'd been a pale Rose. It was a perverted sort of lust, he knew that; a lust for the poison of hatred that was in her; for the Rose with the poisonous thorn.

Pat could sense it – that, somehow, she had a hold on him and that he lusted after something in her; something of evil and of hatred in her. For the first time in her life she felt the thrill of evil, and hot with evil, who had always been cool and kind. She found she wanted to shock; so he'd understand that, in her, he had an accomplice as evil as himself. She said "Helen Leston still trusts me. She'll come here to visit me if I persuade her – I wonder if you've still got your old power to fascinate her?"

He tensed-up at what she was saying, and it reminded Pat of the way he used to stand at the tennis net, ready to spring. He was tense, and rigid, with his rod rigid, and as full of sap as Aaron's rod; and thirsting to drink from the poisoned spring of hate. He said "Helen hates me."

Pat said "Of course she hates you... but what if she desires you still? – What a victory that would be, over the Blackshirt! For him to be cuckolded by a Jew!" She laughed, and lay back, across the bed like a wanton, and Gerald felt his rod swell for her, with sap, like Aaron's rod. He leaned across her, and held her breasts in his hands, with his rod hard-up against her. He said "Hold me hard! Hold me!" and she gripped him. She reached down with her hand, and held him; her fingers on him were as soft as rose-petals, and her nails like a delicious prick of thorns.

He was panting with the excitement of it, and he said "Squeeze! – Pull and squeeze!" He took one hand, away from her breast, and he touched her, there, where her secret thorn was hard; not gently, but deliberately rough, he nipped her, there, with his nails, as if to nip the thorn. The sensation made her jolt, and her reaction was to squeeze so hard, he was nearly forced to cry "Enough!"; but, instead, he thrust his own finger deep, like a gardener preparing a rose-bed.

"You're hurting!" she said, and he answered "You'd like me to hurt Helen Leston, wouldn't you?"

She said "You've hurt her so much already, but, yes, I want you to hurt her again."

He said "Do you want me now, Pat? Are you ready for my rod?"

"Yes!" she said "Yes" and she was panting.

"The sap rose in Aaron's rod, and it blossomed" Gerald said.

"I want to feel the rod" she said, and, as she spoke, the cupboard door swung wide. The sun was low against the side of the house, and it beamed bright, through the crack in the wall, like a gash of lightning.

Gerald gave her the rod: deep; with a lovely shock deep

into her, like lightning going deep to earth. She tensed with the thrill of it, in the way that the victim tenses at the first jolt of the chair. She felt she wanted to shout-out, with the thrill of it, but no shout came.

Gerald jolted once more, then held the rod, deep, where she could feel it, as the picador holds the lance, deep into the bull. For Gerald it was the thrill of power, potency, and for Pat the intense thrill of it was almost pain. It made her so wild, she reached round his neck, and pulled him down, with her mouth greedy for his mouth; open for his tongue and her teeth sharp: sharp as thorns, to draw blood. He felt the intoxicating lust of her, as though he'd absorbed some maddening poison from her bite, and, in turn, his own teeth drew blood. He pulled his mouth free and said "We're blood-brother-and-sister now! The Rose and the Star, united in blood, against the Swastika."

The thrusts and jolts were coming harder now, and fast. Her instinct made her move with them to meet them; and to push hard against the iron, like the bull. "Ah!" she shouted "Ah!" as the lance's last thrust pierced her; as the rod's last jolt struck water; as the sap of the rod brought forth blossom, and mingled with the waters of the well.

They lay together, in mutual exhaustion, and Pat tasted the salt-taste of their mingled blood on her lip. She said "We've shared our blood, like you said: the Rose and the Star against the Swastika."

"It's not only our blood that's mingled" he replied "The sap of the rod is united with the waters of the well."

Pat telephoned Helen at her home. The first time she rang, she got Tim on the line. When she heard his voice, the poison in her burned like fever, and she put the receiver down without speaking. The next time, she did get Helen on the line, and she forced herself to sound all sugary, as though she'd forgotten all about the crack in the wall – and wasn't it a pity that Helen, her best friend, had never even seen her pretty cottage? Helen was suspicious, naturally – that Pat Curry should be so sugary after all the accusations she'd made about Tim. But Pat said that she didn't see why they should let it spoil their friendship, and she'd love Helen to come and see the cottage. There would be no need to tell Tim about it, and Pat would come round and collect Helen, in her car.

Helen was still suspicious, but, really, what could be the harm? She'd been so lonely, not ever seeing her best friend. Tim would be out for the rest of the day on a survey, and anything was better than an empty afternoon, alone.

Pat was at Helen's house within the hour, and was soon fussing over Helen as though nothing had ever come between them, not even Tim. She showed Helen over the cottage, even the room with the crack, though she'd made sure that the cupboard door was closed. Then they sat together in the room overlooking the garden, with the french doors open to the sun, and to the scent of English roses. Pat served tea, and it reminded Helen of when she'd been so happy at the club, before the accident.

The doorbell rang, and Pat went to the door. She spoke loudly, so that Helen could hear "You'll never guess who's here, Gerald: an old friend of yours, Helen Leston."

Gerald! – the name brought a stab of agony and of panic, and Helen wanted to run; to run anywhere, through the open french door, and away. But she couldn't run, not since the accident; and now she couldn't even move. It was as if all the old, terrible paralysis had returned; just as it had been when she'd been left in the ditch, like a dog. All she could do was to grip the arm of her chair, and to look away, into the garden. Gerald was in the room now, and he was saying "What a delightful surprise!" Then he turned to Pat, and said "I was one of Helen's many admirers, Pat – at the tennis club, do you remember? Helen Pringle was the belle of the club!"

Helen kept staring into the garden, and ignoring him, so

he went round, in front of her where she couldn't help but see how he was smiling. He said "You're still the belle, I see, Helen."

She was flushed with anger, and hardly able to speak. "The belle! The belle" she managed to say "You were always a flatterer Gerald Rinkman! A flatterer with a forked tongue."

He bowed his head in contrition "I was young and selfish – I'm ashamed, Helen. But now, I've seen so much pain – the death-camps; the gas-chambers – I don't expect you to forgive me, Helen."

He'd come here out of hatred, to flatter with a forked tongue, and even to cuckold the Blackshirt. But now this poor woman whom he'd ditched like a dog, had touched his heart again, in the same way that his heart had been touched with pity at the gates of Belsen. He said, and he meant what he said "I'm so glad that you made such a recovery, Helen; a miraculous recovery. I'm glad that you're still the belle!"

Pat noticed his tone of voice, and that it was sincere, and she noticed the tear in Helen's eye. It made her jealous to see it, and she was tempted to abort the whole plot. But she hated Tim Leston even more than she was jealous of Helen. She hated Tim enough, even, to risk Helen and Gerald rediscovering their love; she'd even risk that for the chance of the Blackshirt being cuckolded by the Jew. She said "I have to go out for a while. Do you mind if I leave you two together?" and she went outside to her car, and drove away.

Pat hadn't even bothered to offer a plausible pretext. She wanted to show Helen up as a bitch who'd come running back to lick her Master, who'd callously kicked her into a ditch.

Helen said "I wish I could forgive you Gerald. The shock of what you saw in Germany will have aroused pity in anyone; even you."

He said "I've not been happy, Helen. I married the wrong girl. I married a Jewess, when I should have married an

English Rose."

"Pat Curry's an English rose" she said.

Gerald made a dismissive gesture with his hands that was very Jewish; it brought back to Helen how attractive she used to find these Jewish mannerisms of his, and the way he had the warm touch of the Levant. He said "Pat's a wilted rose, Helen; a wilted, pale, tea-rose. I lost my red Rose forever."

Helen's heart was touched, in spite of all the bitterness and the pain. She said "You didn't lose your rose. You threw it away."

He said "If only I hadn't been such a fool as to throw away my red rose."

He'd intended to be cynical, and he'd even rehearsed what he was going to say to Helen, and he'd planned the way he'd try to seduce her. He had not even contemplated his heart being touched. He decided to be bold. He said "Do you remember the wonderful way we used to make love, Helen? Do you think the red rose could ever bloom for me again?"

Helen felt confused, and amazed at herself that she didn't scream out at him to leave her alone. He had his hand on hers and he was leading her, out of the room, and upstairs, to the room where the crack was hidden behind the cupboard door.

They looked out across the garden, and after a while, he said "Do you remember when we looked-out, over the lake by moonlight?"

She said "I remember" and the memory was wonderful, now that she was allowing herself the memory again. She said "But the bad time – the terrible time. It happened so soon afterwards, Gerald."

He said "I can't expect you to forgive me, Helen."

They sat on the edge of the bed, side by side, and he took her hand again. He said "I never stopped loving you, Helen. I was a coward, that's all."

She said "Are you still a coward, Gerald?"

"No" he said "I had to prove to myself that I'm not a coward, in the war."

She was tired – she still got tired from even a little exertion; even from climbing the stairs. She lay back, on the bed, and she wondered if she was half-dreaming, amazed at herself that she could so lightly put-aside half a lifetime of hating Gerald Rinkman, and thus betray Tim, her husband, to his enemy.

Gerald touched her, gently and lovingly, and, when she was ready, he took her gently and with a kind of reverence. "My rose" he whispered "My red, red rose."

When they went downstairs the tea had grown cold, and, soon, Pat returned. Pat saw how they were looking at one another, Helen and Gerald, and she knew. Oh, she'd hoped it would happen; that her enemy the Blackshirt would be cuckolded by the Jew. But love? That the two should fall in love again? She felt jealousy and cold anger, and hate; and an empty despair that this, the only man who'd ever noticed her, had taken her from behind the teacups for nothing more than lust. She said "I'm afraid that I'll have to take you home, Helen. If you've finished your tea."

Outside, in the hall, Pat said "I hope you like my little cottage, Helen."

"Oh, Pat, it's perfect" Helen said "You're so lucky."

"I love this cottage more than anything in the world" Pat said, speaking loudly so that Gerald should overhear "I can hardly bear to show you its faults; but it does have a terrible fault, Helen – Come I'll show you."

She led Helen up the staircase and when she indicated the little bedroom Helen had a panic feeling that Pat knew what had happened in the bedroom and was going to confront her. Pat opened the cupboard door, and there was the cruel gash. "Oh, Pat!" Helen exclaimed "How terrible!"

"It is terrible" said Pat "I feel like a mother with a sick child, who can't rest until her child is well again."

CHAPTER FIFTEEN

Gerald's heart was so touched by Helen that he was almost tempted, for her sake, to let the Fascist keep his pound of flesh. But then he remembered the black shirts of the camp guards, and the horror of the victims in the camps. So he wrote a formal solicitor's letter to T. Leston Esq, Fellow of the Royal Institute of Chartered Surveyors. He enclosed a copy of the independent surveyor's Report and he wrote that the report clearly indicated Mr. Leston's negligence. He also enclosed the builder's estimate, and asked Tim kindly to inform him of the name of his Insurers.

When Tim didn't reply – and Gerald had never really expected a reply – Gerald served a Writ for Damages.

Tim knew he was cornered, "It's that damned Jew again" he shouted "He'll never give up until he's taken his pound of flesh from my heart."

Tim had said nothing to Helen, about Pat's cottage and the gash in the wall; but he'd no need to explain. Helen couldn't risk him knowing she'd seen the gash. She felt so knotted-up, and so betrayed by Gerald yet again, for sending Tim the solicitor's letter. Gerald had told her that he still loved her, but, whether it was love or not, his hatred for Tim was stronger than any love. She whispered "If only you hadn't let your Insurance lapse, Tim."

"Insurance!" he shouted. He was raving, now, with that intense, mad look that frightened Helen. She feared that this, latest, crisis might finally tip Tim's precarious mental balance over into insanity.

"Insurance!" he kept-on shouting "The Insurance Companies are all run by the Jews! – the Jews have got their grip on everything. Rinkman, the Jew, wants to destroy me, Helen."

She said "I'll go and see him, Tim. I'll plead with him. He may be kind, for my sake."

"Don't you dare!" he shouted, and then, with a kind of mad intuition, he screamed "You haven't been seeing him, have you Helen? You haven't betrayed me to the Jews?"

She was crying and saying "I've seen Pat... I've been so lonely Tim, and Pat was my last, best friend."

"She's as bad as Rinkman!" he shouted "She could have chosen any other lawyer in Liverpool. Why do you think she picked the Jew? It's a conspiracy, Helen, don't you see? Pat Curry's a false friend; as bad as the Jew."

She tried to interrupt him, but he ignored her distress. He jumped-up, from his chair, and began to pace about the room, gesticulating, with the Writ, and Gerald's earlier letter in his hand. "Never forget the way the Jew dumped you in a ditch, like a dog! And remember who it was who saved you. – I pulled you out of the ditch, Helen. Oh, the ambulance men might have pulled your broken body out, but it was I who rescued your spirit. I nursed you, and I made you walk again, Helen. Never forget that."

"How could I forget?" she managed to force the words out, through her sobs "But Pat was always loyal. You drove Pat away, Tim. You drove her into Gerald Rinkman's arms."

"Well!" he shouted "Well! – Your two friends are both now our enemies! Lovers, too, I shouldn't wonder." He spoke with cruel intuition; he knew just how to hurt.

All her hopes and disappointments were racing through Helen's mind – how wonderful it would have been if there had never been that car-crash, and she'd married her Prince Charming and been happy ever after. She remembered how, only a short time ago, her Prince had come back to her, and had re-awakened her like Sleeping Beauty; and now, so soon afterwards, he was betraying her once more! It all went to show that he couldn't really love her: it must all have been deceit, and a cruel plot, with Pat her best friend in it too – and yet; and yet... He'd called her his red, red rose, and, in his shallow way, she knew that he did love her. And what of Pat, her loyal friend? – Gerald's love had always been shallow, but Pat's friendship had been deep.

Gerald knew very well that, if he took his pound of flesh, and made the Blackshirt suffer, Helen would suffer too. He'd forced himself to harden his heart, but now, because Helen was his red rose again he was tempted to relent. It worried him so much that he drove out to Woolton, to talk it over with Pat.

Pat said "It's not easy for you to meet Helen; that's the only reason you're still bothering with me." She was bitter about it, and it was true.

Gerald said "I cuckolded the Fascist – that's what you wanted, wasn't it?"

Pat said "I wanted you to hurt Helen – not to love her."

He said "Revenge against the Fascist – that's what binds you and me together Pat. The Star of David and the White Rose united against the Swastika – that's what makes our passion so intense."

She was hating him for loving Helen, but still she was on fire for him. She'd been longing for true love, but all she could hope to get from him was lust: a furnace of lust, stoked by mutual hatred of their enemy. She said "I used to admire Helen, but now I despise her. She's like a little bitch who keeps nuzzling up to her master, even after he's kicked her into a ditch."

Gerald said "I'm not proud of the way I treated Helen."

"Come then!" she said "Come with me to the room with the crack – the same room where your little bitch nuzzled-up to you."

He went with her, and she was wild for him. At first he was reluctant, and he wondered how the modest girl behind the

183

teacups could have become so brazen. His reluctance maddened her even more, and she taunted him as a harlot might have taunted him. She threw-off all her clothes, and pulled at his clothes, to make him hurry, until they were standing there, together, naked. Then she gripped his rod, and, still standing, she stood tiptoe and over the rod and squeezed it, to feel the taut tip of the rod where it touched the tiny thorn of the rose.

The violent movement caused them to overbalance, onto the bed, and he was there, on the bed beside her, with the rod erect. Pat twisted and straddled him, and sat-back on the rod, to feel him, deep. Gerald was now as wild as she, with his hands up, and cupping her breasts; and she was pressing down on him, to press her whole weight on him, and to feel him, hard. Then, she was leaning over him, with her hands on his chest, and her hair damp with sweat. For a while they stayed that way, motionless, like an obscene tableau; and it gave Gerald an extra thrill of lust that the demure girl - behind-the-teacups should behave for him like a whore of Amsterdam.

For no apparent reason, the cupboard-door creaked, and swung open, just as it has swung wide that other time – as if there was some occult force, some force of hatred, in the lightning-gash. They both turned at the sound, and it made Pat mad to see the cruel crack."Look!" she snarled, "The Fascist and the Fascist's wife – that's what they've done to me, Gerald" and, wildly, she began to twist on him, as though she was on horseback, and her nails dug into his chest, where they pressed.

She was jumping now, and rising; rising and jumping, and he was rising to her – as wild as she, now, and his rod swollen with lust: as hard as a lance and thrust forward in the charge! and, yes, thrust deep; deep and forward into the enemy – deep into the Fascist enemy, with the last, deep thrust of death.

They lay back together, exhausted; like victorious

184

comrades, lying together, anywhere, on the battlefield: anywhere, on top of the dead, even, in the deep exhaustion of victory.

At last Gerald said "You didn't give me time to say what I came here to say." And, when she didn't reply, he went on "Helen was your friend. She was my friend, as well. We should be generous, for Helen's sake."

Pat was amazed, and angry "If you give-in to Helen, you give-in to the Swastika as well."

"Helen's on my conscience" Gerald said.

But Pat was unmoved. She felt no pity, or any feeling for Helen at all, except for jealousy that Gerald should love her. She said "Helen stood aside while her husband swindled me – in the same way that he swindled all her friends."

"I know" Gerald said "But still, I owe her a debt, for the way I ditched her."

"My God, Gerald!" Pat exclaimed "You're so sentimental, and I always thought you were strong."

Gerald said "I now believe that Tim Leston is mad – really mad in the clinical sense. He'll go to Court against us and lose. He'll not only have to pay for all the building work himself, not being Insured, but there will be Legal Costs as well. It will break him Pat. I know that's what we both want, but it will break Helen as well."

"What's your idea then, Mister Sentimental?"

"Why not offer him a let-out?" Gerald said "Let him pay half the total building costs. There'll be no Legal Costs if we settle out of Court."

She was too angry to protest. "How nice for me, to pay the other half" she said sarcastically.

"I'll pay" said Gerald "I owe it to Helen. I'll pay."

Gerald's letter to Tim was as tactful as he could make it. He knew he was dealing with a man even prouder than Antonio, for Tim would never accept a favour from a Jew.

Gerald explained that, if Tim had allowed his Indemnity Insurance to lapse, Gerald's client was prepared, without prejudice, to share the building costs.

This letter, as far as Tim was concerned, was even worse than an insult: it was a letter full of pity, from a Jew. For a Blackshirt, a whiff of Jewish pity was more pungent even than the smoke of gas-ovens.

"Damn the Jew!" he shouted at poor Helen, who was nowadays his only audience. "The damned Jew dares to offer me his charity."

"Take it, Tim, oh, please!" Helen begged. "Somehow, we'll raise the money for half the building costs. Another lot of Legal costs would break us, Tim. I'd have to sell the house."

But he wasn't listening; he was raving-mad. "Give-in to the Jew?" he shouted "Never! – Give-in and pay-up to the Jew and his Harlot? – Never!"

"Stop-it!" Helen was angry now. "You mustn't say such things about Pat." She was all tense, and on the defensive, as if, somehow, Tim might find a way to penetrate the defences of her own mind, and that he might suspect her own reawakened love for Gerald. She was frightened to support Gerald's offer too enthusiastically. She'd given-in to Gerald, and she was weak, but there was one thing she knew for certain now: if Gerald loved any woman at all, then that woman was herself. He didn't love Pat: Pat had chosen the harlot's role. She said "You're cruel, Tim. You mustn't say such things about Pat."

He said "Let the Jew and the Harlot sue for damages! – I'll never pay."

Gerald waited in vain for a reply from Tim, and he wondered how he could speak to Helen without Tim knowing. He waited in his car near to Helen's house around the corner up the lane, until he saw Tim drive away. Then he drove to his own office, and telephoned Helen. He said "Helen – the offer to pay half the building costs – the offer doesn't really come from Pat. It comes from me, Helen. It's not really for Tim at all – it's from me to you. I owe it to you, Helen. Tim must never know it comes from me."

Helen said "I'm grateful, Gerald. But money can't ever make up for what you did to me."

"I know" he said "I want you to know – the other day, when we were together... there's still some decency left in me, Helen. Some love."

She found she was crying, and hardly able to speak. "Do you love Pat, too?" she said.

"Pat?" he replied "Pat and I – that's only a business arrangement."

Helen said "When Tim got your letter he went raving mad. He won't accept your offer, Gerald."

"Pat's offer" he corrected her "As far as Tim's concerned."

"Pat's offer, but your pity" she said "Tim won't take pity from a Jew."

"What more can I do?" Gerald said. And Helen had no answer.

Helen made one, last plea to Tim. She said "How can Gerald be sure you're not insured, Tim? – Pay half the building costs and say it's from your Insurance Company." But it was no good. It had gone beyond mere financial considerations; Tim would never bring himself to accepting charity from a Jew.

Tim's laugh was dry and bitter. He said "Don't delude yourself, Helen. The Jew knows I'm not Insured... Just as Shylock knew that Antonio's ship would never come to harbour."

Helen said "A pound of flesh from the heart is worth far more to us than half the building costs. Pay him off, Tim! Pay him off, for my sake."

Tim said, and his tone was threatening "I believe you've still got a soft spot for the Jew, Helen. Even now, after he ditched you like a dog. After all the bitterness and the pain."

It was too close to the mark, and she was frightened. If ever Tim turned against her, she knew he'd exact a penalty as terrible as Shylock's. "I hate Gerald Rinkman" she lied "But I'm afraid of fighting him – if I have to lose this house it would be like losing a pound of flesh from my heart."

Tim was immovable "If I agreed to pay-up Rinkman would win the final victory. Gerald Rinkman ditched you, Helen, and I picked you up, out of the ditch. If I paid-up now, it would be like paying for something he values less than a dead dog."

Helen could hardly speak, to protest against his twisted reasoning. She was tense and her eyes full of tears as she managed to say "That's cruel Tim – but why was it that you bothered to lift me out of the ditch?" – She'd never dared to say it, but she said it now; she had to stop him, somehow, from allowing her heart to be torn-out to save his pride. "I was broken, Tim; broken and worthless. But it wasn't only me that you wanted, was it? It was daddy's money."

"Quiet!" he shouted, but she dared to go-on. Nothing could stop the flood, now that the dam had burst. "Where is daddy's money now, Tim? – Gone! All gone. All gone, in trying to show that you're a bigger man than Gerald Rinkman." She was hysterical, and the words were coming out between the sobs "All gone, trying to prove that no Jew can ever be bigger than you, when, really, you're no bigger than a Jew – You've always known that your grandmother was Jewish, haven't you?"

Her flood of tears abated, and Tim said "I've sacrificed my life for you, Helen. I've spent my life looking after you, when I could have been big. I've sacrificed my success, to be your nurse."

Helen said "That's your great excuse, isn't it Tim? – that, and your crusade against the Jews. Those have been your excuses for your failure. If it hadn't been for daddy's money, your inadequacy would have been obvious, long ago."

It was the truth, and the truth hurt so much that he raised his hand, and she thought he would strike her. He shouted "It was your own fault, Helen! You were even more full of pride than I was. You couldn't bear your husband to look inferior to the Jew who'd ditched you."

She knew it was the truth. She might have denied it, but the flood had washed-away all self-deceit. She said "We've both been full of pride, Tim. But do we have to suffer eternal damnation for our pride, like Lucifer? – pay your half-share of the building-costs! Please, Tim. For Mercy's sake, pay!"

"Mercy?" he exclaimed "Mercy?" Again, he was suspicious "Have you been begging for mercy, Helen? For mercy from the Jew?"

She said "Gerald Rinkman's not as bad as Shylock, Tim. Shylock refused to show mercy – Gerald is being merciful."

Tim said "A Jew never gives something for nothing – just what did you offer him, Helen?"

Again, he was too close to the mark, and she couldn't hide her nervousness, as he went on "Just by visiting Pat Curry you were a traitor to me, Helen."

She said "How was I to know that Gerald Rinkman would be there?"

"So!" he said "I was right in my suspicion."

"Pay the half-share of the building-costs" she begged him, "Why not?"

He jumped-up, and took her shoulder, to turn her towards the french-window, and, through it, to the Jewish Refugees' Home that loomed so close. "There's your answer!" he shouted "How could I ever accept mercy from the Jew after that?"

"You'll be in Court again, Tim" she whispered "I don't

think I can face it all, again."

"I must defend myself, Helen!" he argued "I have to vindicate myself in public. – The Jew has accused me of negligence: of professional incompetence. If I pay him now, and so, tacitly, admit he's right, I'll be ashamed for ever."

"Oh, Tim!" she was crying again "People say that you're addicted to litigation. They say you're drunk with litigation – some people are addicted to litigation, like alcohol. This will be the third court-case, Tim."

He tried to shout her down, in an attempt to stop the flow, but the last dyke of her reticence was breached by the flood of truth. "The third court-case" she went on "With people sniggering at the way you go-on about Jews... I can't bear it, Tim. Sometimes I wonder if you're unbalanced, the way you go-on."

He said "You'll never understand.... A Blackshirt must never knuckle-under to a Jew."

CHAPTER SIXTEEN

Gerald gave Tim a month to reply. After only a few days he knew that there would be no response, but still, he gave Tim a month.

At the end of the month he wrote again to Tim, that it would be dangerous further to delay the building works, and he instructed the builder to proceed with the job.

When the works were completed, Gerald arranged for the builder to be paid. He sent a copy of the receipted invoice to Tim, with a covering letter, repeating the offer to settle out of Court without prejudice. When there was still no response from Tim, Gerald served a writ in the full sum of the building costs.

Tim didn't get a chance to repeat his tour de force of the Libel action, when he'd used the High Court as a platform for his anti-Semitism. This, the latest case, was unsensational. Although the sum involved was too great for the County Court, the hearing in an empty High Court, before a Judge without a Jury, was dull routine, and all the evidence was technical. It was far too dry to interest the public, or to feature on the front pages of newspapers. It was inevitable that the Judge would find for the Plaintiff, Miss Pat Curry, and he ordered the Defendant, Tim Leston to pay damages in the full sum, and to meet the total costs of the case.

This time Helen didn't even try to plug the dyke; she was in despair. The years of her loyal support for Tim were over: all the years when he'd taken advantage of her friends for money; all the years when she'd cringed in silence while he ranted-on against Jews, until, now, the only audience for his ranting was herself; all the years when, because she was so dependant on him, she'd smiled in humble support, when, really, she longed to protest; all the years when he was spending her father's money – her money – to aggrandize himself.

Tim was saying "I'm afraid we'll have to sell the house; it's the only way."

She'd stopped crying: she was cold, now, and beyond tears "Would you turn us out into the street, Tim?"

But he was still vain; still full of himself. "Now, Helen" he said "How can you imagine that a man with my contacts could be out on the street? A man who's respected at Sykes-Waterhouse? – This house will fetch a good price, I'll make sure of that. We'll buy another house, a good house, at half the price... A master-surveyor like myself can get the best out of property."

"A surveyor like you, Tim?" she was bitter enough to attack him with sarcasm "A surveyor who didn't even notice a crack like forked-lightning? A surveyor who neglected even to insure himself?"

She'd touched the raw nerve of his professional pride, and his arm was raised as if to strike her; but she didn't care. She no longer felt afraid of him, and she spoke coldly "I'll never agree to sell this house, Tim."

He said "The house may be in your name, but so is the mortgage. There's no prospect, now, of meeting the mortgage repayments. The house will be repossessed, Helen."

She said "I could end-up hating you, Tim. You made me sell all daddy's shares, and spend all his money. And, now, because of your pride and your court-cases, I'm going to lose daddy's house."

He said "I've told you: there are other houses."

"No!" she screamed "No! – my only other remaining asset is my Life Insurance; the one that daddy took-out for me. But it doesn't mature for years... They won't pay-out for years, Tim, unless I die... If I die, they pay-up right away... Ironic, isn't it? – the only way I can save my house is if I'm dead."

She felt suddenly tired, the way she'd not felt for years,

Oh! since that time after her terrible accident, when she'd been ditched like a dog; when it had made her tired to walk a little way, even with a crutch. She said "I'm so tired, Tim. So tired I can't think. I must go upstairs to bed."

He was full of concern for her: it had become a habit, he'd been concerned for her for so long. He said "Let me help you upstairs, Helen."

"No, please, Tim" she replied "I mustn't give-in. If I give-in it will be like that terrible time, all over again."

He looked at her, and he seemed to be examining her closely, but, really, his mind was on the Jew, and whether, somehow, he could work-out a plan to best him. He said, "I'll stay downstairs for a bit. I've some ideas to work-out."

"Goodnight, Tim" Helen said, and, if he'd not been so distracted he'd have thought it curious that she should wish him goodnight, when he would shortly be following her upstairs.

As she made her way upstairs she was smiling, and almost happy, like someone who's found a simple solution to an insoluble problem. She went to her dressing table, and took-out the few papers that she still kept private to herself: the letter from daddy, when he'd gone away on business that time – she had so few letters from daddy because he'd hardly ever gone away and left her: the photograph of daddy and mummy on their wedding day; not much else, not even the deeds of the house, which were kept in the bank which held the mortgage. But what she did have was the Insurance Policy on her life. It wasn't a complicated policy: provided the premium payments were kept-up, the policy paid-out on maturity, or death. There was a short list of conditions, and one of these was an exclusion clause for suicide.

She left the Policy, open, on her dressing table; then she climbed the next flight of stairs to the attic landing.

She looked down, over the bannister. She'd left the stairwell lights on deliberately, and, two floors below, the hallway was lit-up like the nave of a church. She felt no fear – just a deep regret for what might have been, and for everything that had happened since the day she'd nearly died in the ditch.

She looked down; deep down into the heart of her house: the house that was more valuable to her even than life. She leaned over, far over the rail, and the height made her dizzy. She'd heard how heights could attract people, down, into the depths, into the deep heart of the depths; and she went-over, over the rail, and down, down, deep into the heart of the house she loved.

She did not scream. And, when Tim heard the sound, it was a dull thud, a dead sound, like an extra-heavy thud in his heart.

He knew. He went out into the bright light of the hallway, and there she was; with her head smashed, and a smile on her face. He said "You didn't have to do it, Helen. The Jew isn't worth your life." He moved towards the telephone to summon help, but she was still able to speak. "No, Tim," she whispered.

He said "An ambulance – I must call an ambulance. You jumped deliberately!"

Her voice was still audible "No" she whispered urgently "An accident: that's important, Tim. If it was deliberate, the Insurance wouldn't pay."

"Insurance?" he said foolishly.

"I told you I'd die rather than sell the house" she said "The Insurance will cover it: an accident – remember!"

The shock of seeing her there, all broken, had numbed him, but it gave way to panic. "No!" he shouted "An ambulance!"

"Silly" she whispered. Her voice had nearly gone "It's your house, now, Tim. Don't sell the house; never sell."

She died, and he knew that to call an ambulance was pointless: there was more urgent business for a Blackshirt than pointlessly to call an ambulance.

He stood there, in the harsh light at the bottom of the stairwell, staring down at the broken doll with the silly smile. He felt no sense of lost love, but he did feel loss – the deep, vindictive, sense of loss of a Blackshirt who's been cheated of his girl, by a Jew. Little man as he was, he stood tall, and, thrusting his arm he shouted "Heil Hitler! Sieg Heil!"

He stamped up the staircase, and on, past the lower landing and up to the attic. He looked over the rail, down into the stairwell and the hallway all lit-up, and at the broken doll with the silly smile. Then he kicked open the door to the attic bedroom in the way the Gestapo used to kick open bedroom doors, and he wrenched-open the wardrobe door.

It was all there; every precious item was there, and ready, as it was always ready. That was one thing Helen never failed to do, he thought grimly. She never failed to keep it all ready, in case the Leader's summons came. Oh, how it fascinated her! – How she loved to see him in his uniform, and how wild and sensuous it made her! As for himself, it had always made him feel big and dominant: sexually powerful, to master her, and to be the Blackshirt master. He spoke out-loud "Only a Blackshirt can smash the Jew!"

He undressed, and stood naked in front of the mirror. He was aroused and hard as an S.S. dagger, standing there: aroused by the sight of the black uniform in the cupboard, which he worshipped like some pagan idol in a tabernacle. He took the black shirt and put it on; he put it on with reverence like a priest putting-on a vestment. Then the trousers: not the plain trousers of a Blackshirt in the ranks, but the grey-black jodhpurs of a Blackshirt officer, like Mosley. He pulled-on the jodhpurs, and picked-up the boots; the black jackboots. How lovingly Helen had polished them, with a deep shine; and, if you looked deep into the shine, you could see what might have been a swastika, and the shadow of a million jackboots, stamping, stamping, over the piteous faces of Jews.

"Sieg Heil!" he shouted, and he wished that his poor, broken wife was still alive, to pull-on the jackboots for him, the way she loved to do it.

He pulled-on the boots himself, and tied the tie – not for him the ranker's open-neck; – then he put on the tunic, that was like an army-officer's service-dress, only black, and he buckled-on the belt. Last of all, he put on the cap. He put it on carefully, the way Sir Oswald Mosley wore his cap, with the peak low, over the eyes. On his arm was sewn the lightning-flash, proud badge of the British Union.

He was ready. He stood erect and still; worshipping the image of himself reflected in the mirror; resplendent in the sacred uniform of Sir Oswald Mosley, his god.

"Sieg Heil!" he shouted, and thrust his arm, and clicked his heels together. "Helen worshipped her Blackshirt!" he shouted again "Heil Hitler!" And he stamped across the room, in a slow goose-step.

"Death to the Jews!" he shouted, and stamped down the stairs, and past the broken doll with the silly smile. Then he got into his car, and drove away, with a roar, into the night.

He was cunning. He knew that, if Pat Curry saw him, dressed like that after dark, outside her front door, she would refuse to let him in. So he stopped, and put-on his raincoat to cover his uniform, and took-off his cap. He rang the bell, and Pat called-out "Who's that? – It's late."

She was nervous, and Tim forced himself to sound normal "It's only Tim Leston. I must speak to you urgently, Pat."

She hesitated, but then she thought – perhaps he's seen sense, at last; perhaps he's decided to give-in. So she opened the door to him; she felt she owed it to the husband of her oldest friend. She'd been worried about Helen, after the court-case, and she said "How's Helen, Tim?"

"Dead!" he said. He was taking-off his raincoat and hanging it on a coathook, and, next to it, he was hanging his cap.

"Dead?" Pat said, still not comprehending "You can't mean dead, Tim?"

"Sieg Heil!" he shouted, and clicked his heels.

It frightened Pat; she'd never have thought she could be frightened of Tim Leston, who everyone used to laugh at, at the tennis club, even after he became one of Mosley's Blackshirts. "Tiger Tim" they used to call him behind his back, after the comic paper-tiger in the strip-cartoon. But now she was really frightened; it wasn't just the uniform, it was something about the mad look in his eyes, and she began to believe that Helen really was dead, and that Tim had killed her.

Even in his madness, Tim noticed that there was something unfamiliar about Pat, something that in a faded rose was almost bizarre: this wasn't the usual dowdy girl behind the teacups; she was painted like a harlot, and scented with the sweet, heavy scent of lust. It raised his own lust, and his hate, all at once; lust and hate together. Tim knew the answer instinctively: Pat was all made-up, and waiting for her lover, for Gerald Rinkman: full of lust for the Jew, and eager to be his harlot. "Whore!" he shouted "Jew-lover!"

She tried to placate him. "You're not well, Tim. Let me call a doctor."

But he got to the 'phone before her, and wrenched-out the wires. "You were going to call the police" he said "But it was you who really killed Helen. You and the Jew."

He was mad; completely demented and dangerous, she was certain of it. She moved suddenly, to try to get out of the door, and to make a run for it. But he grabbed hold of her, and, when she fought to get away, he was surprisingly strong; as if the uniform had given him unnatural strength.

She scratched at him, and struggled; and, when she

tried to scream, he put his hand across her mouth. She was
fighting him, now, and struggling for her life, and kicking-out,
to make him lose his grip. His eyes were close to her eyes, and
looking deep into the terror he found there. It excited him, and
made him want to dominate her, in the way he'd loved to
dominate Helen, when he was in his uniform. He remembered
the newsreels they'd shown during the war, of Hitler's S.S. and
how each recruit had to strangle his pet dog: to make his heart
oblivious to pity each recruit had to strangle his canine friend
to death. It had excited Tim, the whole idea of it, and the
propaganda film that was meant to harden British hearts
against the Nazis had had the opposite effect on him. It excited
him now and aroused him sexually, so that, with a manic grip,
he grasped Pat by the throat, and shook her while he squeezed.
She gave one scream, a short shriek, and then she gurgled and
went limp.

She still breathed: she was insensible, but still she
breathed. It excited Tim to see her like that: she the slave and
he the master. He was hard: hard as an S.S. dagger and as
cruel. He was tearing at her; tearing at her knickers, under her
skirt, and tearing her flesh there with his nails. He ripped the
pants away, then he unbuckled his belt, and thrust his fleshy
dagger, deep; all hard and cruel he thrust, and thrust again until
his poor, limp victim half awoke and gave a moan.

"Jew-lover!" he spat, and delivered his last, deep, coup
de grace.

She was really awake now, but not struggling or
screaming; only moaning. He was deep inside her, with his
dagger limp, and, looking into her, he felt no pity. "Jew-lover!"
he spat again, and tightened his grip on her throat. She didn't
resist; she had no will left to resist. She just looked pitifully at
him, and died.

Tim stood away from her, then he went upstairs to find
a full-length mirror: a Blackshirt officer on duty couldn't let the

Leader down, and Tim still had Blackshirt duty to complete. He tidied his hair and re-buckled his belt; then, satisfied, "Sieg Heil!" he shouted and thrust his arm.

A lipstick on the dressing-table caught his eye. On impulse, he took the lipstick, and, on the newly-built wall, where the cupboard and the lightning-crack had been, he drew, in blood-red lipstick, a Swastika and Lightning-Flash.

He laughed.

"Death to all Jews!" he shouted "Sieg Heil!"

He went downstairs and took his raincoat and his cap. He put-on the cap, but he carried the raincoat in his hand, back to his car.

Everyone knew where Gerald Rinkman lived: Gerald liked everyone to know. It was one of the big houses overlooking Gateacre Brow; an opulent house, set in its own grounds, behind trees. The drive was lit-up by electric lanterns, and every window of the house blazed with light. Gerald Rinkman's house was a beacon in Liverpool, the way a lighthouse is a beacon at sea. The house itself was a beacon, but its surrounding woods were as empty as the ocean, and its lane as lonely as the depths of the sea.

Tim drove his car towards the beacon, and he parked close-by, where he could watch. He knew that he would not have to watch in vain: he'd seen the way Pat Curry had been painted like a harlot, and he knew who she'd been expecting.

Gerald Rinkman finished his evening meal: it was a rich meal with wine, and prepared as only a Jewish housewife can prepare a meal, with as much pride as if it had been Passover.

Gerald placed his knife and fork on his plate, and his napkin on the table. "That was very good, my dear" he said "Thank you." They were the only words he'd spoken throughout the meal; he had nothing else to say. He rose from the table – "I'm going out" he said "I may be late."

His wife nodded: he'd be out visiting one of his girls; one of his Gentile girls. She didn't care about it any more: the housemaid she employed was a Gentile girl, and she despised all Gentile girls the way she despised the housemaid.

Gerald Rinkman had two Gentile women on his mind and they weren't girls at all – they were women and both nearly as old as himself. He'd had plenty of girls, but now there were just these two women, and he needed them both: Helen Leston who had been Helen Pringle, and Helen's friend Pat Curry. Love and lust: he needed both of them; and, looking into his heart, he knew that both – both love and lust – sprang from his hatred of Fascist Blackshirts, and of Nazi Jackboots stamping over Jewish faces.

But tonight wasn't the time for introspection: Gerald had drunk wine, and had eaten well. Tonight was not the time for introspection or for love; tonight was a time for lust, and lust was waiting for him. His lust for Pat Curry – a perverted lust that sprang from hatred – had revived in Gerald the sort of lust that he'd thought had gone forever with his youth. Pat reciprocated his lust so avidly that it was shocking: the self-effacing girl behind the teacups had become insatiable. She'd have welcomed him every night – and every day, too, if he'd wanted that. And she'd do anything he wished, to tempt him. She'd been clumsy at first, but she was quick to learn all the arts of the courtesan. Each time, before his visit, she would shed her dowdy chrysalis, and emerge as gaudy as a butterfly. She bought lipsticks of deep blood-red, and dark eye-shadow; and he brought her perfumes that were strong and sweet as lust.

He taught her how to tease: how to paint her nipples like fire, and to tempt him to suck. She learned to use her lips, to ring his rampant rod with lipstick, and to touch him there with her tongue. One night he said "I'll mount you like a stallion!" and she bent-over willingly on her stomach across the bed; with her legs splayed wide at the edge of the bed, and open for him. She felt his weight on her, like the weight of a stallion; and, like a strong brood-mare she stood for him. She felt his shaft go deep, and she lusted until, with a cry like the cry of the wild horse, it was done.

Another time, he acted the stallion and she the rider, and, naked, he had her ride him, hard down onto the pommel, so that the pommel was deep into her as she rode him as wild and naked as a gypsy, while he rose-up to her, and rose-up again, like a bucking horse.

All these things that he'd taught her were in Gerald's mind that night, as he called "Goodbye" to his Jewish wife, and went out, into the night, lusting after the Gentile. The anticipation so excited him that he was hard already; hard as a high pommel for the Gentile woman.

Gerald still loved cars; that was another passion he'd never lost: his lust for feline cars, that matched his lust for Gentile women. He kept several cars, but his favourite was his Bentley. It was a car as important to him as his first sports car had been: the car that had died in the ditch. The Bentley was the car for the man who'd arrived, where the sports car had been the car for the man who was on his way.

Gerald got into the Bentley and started her. She purred. She, too, was a lioness, a matriarch of the Pride, whose purr was quiet in the night: a more mature lioness, more experienced than the first, and more powerful.

He let-in the clutch, and the lioness moved slow and stealthily, along the bright-lit drive.

The watcher-in-the-dark was hiding like a jackal, and, as the lioness passed-by, the jackal moved-in at her heels.

Strange! thought Gerald – for a car to come-out like that; out of the empty woods. He dismissed the thought: it must have been lovers, he thought, seeking for privacy.

Then, as he came out of the lane and up to the road, where the lane met the road and Gerald had to stop, there was the sound of a car horn behind him, like a jackal's bark, and the jackal that had been at the lioness' heels accelerated around her, and across her, blocking the way.

Gerald was angry. The bloody fool, he thought – it must be a drunk, to drive like that; and he flung-open the Bentley's door so as to get-out, onto the road, and confront the drunk.

The jackal yapped again, and its driver screamed "If you get-out of the car I'll run you down!"

Gerald was really alarmed now – it was worse than a drunk that he'd come-up against; it was a lunatic. But the lunatic's voice was somehow familiar, and he realised with a shock that it was Tim Leston's voice. And there was Tim at the wheel dressed all in black, with a black cap on his head. He might only have been a chauffeur in chauffeur's uniform, but for the homicidal madness of his expression, and the way he was screaming-out hysterically, like a lunatic.

Gerald's fear turned to panic – had it really come to this? Had hatred unbalanced Tim's mind to madness? He tried to force himself to be calm, and to humour Tim. "Oh, it's Tim Leston!" he called-out "That's a silly fancy-dress you're wearing, Tim."

He couldn't have said anything worse: to sneer at the uniform that Tim worshipped in a tabernacle, like a god.

"Sieg Heil!" screamed Tim "Heil Hitler!"

"You're mad!" Gerald shouted back "Hitler's been dead for ten years. Stop your silly games." He was playing for time, to work-out how to get away. He could see that, although he was pinned-in at the front, he could reverse through the gap. He selected reverse gear, let-out the clutch, and, with a roar, the lioness leapt backwards out of the trap, with a bound; then fast forward, around the nose of the jackal and away, down the brow towards the city-centre of Liverpool. Gerald laughed out-loud in triumph – how could Tim Leston imagine that a car as puny as a jackal could challenge a Bentley with the power of a lioness?

Traffic lights ahead turned to red, and Gerald pulled the lioness to a stop. The jackal screeched up, and pulled in beside her, and the sound Gerald heard might have been the crazy laugh of a hyena. "You – Jew in the Bentley!" Tim was shouting. "A red-light means danger – can you hear me, Jew?"

There were traffic-lights all the way, all the way into Liverpool: down Smithdown road, and Parliament Street; all the way. Gerald had a plan, that was more like an instinct, to drive to the main police station where he'd be safe: the police knew all about dealing with lunatics and locking them up.

The lights changed, and the lioness shot away, leaving the jackal behind. But the next set of lights turned to red, and Tim was screaming, out of the open car window "Cars are your Achilles' Heel, Jew! – Every Achilles has his heel. Even the proud Jew, Rinkman, has his Achilles' heel." He screamed again with a Hyena's laughter; and again Gerald shot ahead. And, again, the next traffic-light was against him.

Tim was still screaming "Remember your flashy, sports car? – That was your Achilles' Heel, Jew! – You couldn't handle that car. You could handle a tennis racket, and manipulate a girl. But you could never handle a car!"

The mocking words were enough to make Gerald as mad as Tim and to want to show how he could master a car in the way he could master everything else. Tim had touched the raw nerve; the raw nerve in the Achilles' Heel. From being in control, and with a rational plan, Gerald was now overcome by Hubris, like Achilles. He'd show the Blackshirt how easy it was for his lioness to shake-off the jackal at her heels!

Gerald was off again, with his foot hard down. Again the lights ahead changed against him, but, this time, Gerald ignored them and drove through against the red. Tim did the same, with Gerald swerving in front of a car coming across

him, and Tim swerving behind it. The Rialto cinema was on
their left at the junction, all lit-up and tawdry, and some people
who'd come out of the cinema had to jump for their lives.
There was a light rain falling, a Mersey mist, and both cars
skidded around the next corner, around the black bulk of the
cathedral and around the deep pit from whence its stone had
been dug.

The near miss had made Gerald shake, so he couldn't
control his car, and he pulled-up at the side of the road. Tim
pulled-up beside him, to give him a full view of the black
uniform under the street-light. "That was dangerous!" Tim
shouted "To crash those lights – wherever you go, Jew, I go
too: through red lights; anywhere."

Gerald was desperate – what could any man do, faced
thus by insanity? He shouted "We can work something out,
Tim. I was on my way to see Pat Curry. Pat wants to be friends
with Helen."

But, again, Tim's answer was the crazy laugh of the
hyena. "Too late!" Came the scream "Your harlot's dead!
Painted and scented for you, and dead!"

Gerald took it as a lie; a trick – it must be. But the
Fascist was still screaming "The harlot's painted and scented! –
Dead and waiting for the Jew." And, again, the night was split
by the hysterical scream of the hyena.

It might just be true! – How else would the Fascist
know Pat's secret? That she played the painted harlot for her
lover? Gerald shouted "Dead? How?"

"With these hands" Tim shouted back, and thrust his
hands at Gerald, through the car window "I strangled the harlot
the way the S.S. used to strangle their pet dogs. To stab or
strangle was the only choice."

Gerald had seen it during the war, on the newsreels,
and now he felt, from out of the darkness of the ages, the
terrible threat of hatred against the Jews. There was one, last,

chance... "Helen is prepared to forgive me" Gerald shouted "Let's both go to Helen."

"Too late again!" and the scream seemed to echo from the sandstone walls of the great church "Helen's dead too – she died rather than let you take her house, Jew."

So – it was finished! There was no way out, now. No other way than Blackshirt against Jew. No other way but to run, or to fight. And Gerald had the car: the lioness with the power! He'd show the Blackshirt who was ring-master, and how he could subject the lioness to his will!

He revved the engine, and flung the steering round; mounting the pavement and away. But, still, he drove in fear, with his hand shaking on the wheel. Why could he never master a car the way he could master a girl?

They were into traffic now, getting into the heart of the city, and that was Gerald's fatal mistake. If he'd headed for the country his speed would have taken him away from Tim. But Gerald had one idea, now, fixed in his mind, to hold-onto; like a castaway who clings to a spar: to drive as quickly as possible to the Central Police Station, and to blast his horn outside.

There were still bombed-sites, more than ten years after the blitz, with rubble bulldozed into heaps to clear a space for parking; and skeletons of buildings awaiting their turn for demolition. They had become so familiar that people no longer noticed them; but Gerald always noticed them. For Gerald they were symbols of menace: symbols as menacing as a Swastika.

The traffic became even thicker, and Gerald's mind was dizzy with fear. There was a jolt, and he'd clipped the side of a tramcar, which shuddered on its tracks, like some great herbivore, hit by a lioness; and another jolt as his wheel hit the kerb. The lioness groaned, but still she bounded forward. She leapt forward, sprang, and stopped, as Gerald stamped first on the accelerator pedal and then on the brake. He felt a bump behind, and there was the jackal still at the lioness' heel, and bumping her. Again, Gerald accelerated, round a bend, and now he was driving anywhere; into back streets, anywhere, to shake-off the jackal. In his panic he'd forgotten his plan to drive to the Police Station; he'd lost his sense of direction, and even lost his mental picture of the Liverpool streets he knew so well.

Here he was now, at the Mersey tunnel entrance, with St. George's Hall above him all solid and inscrutable! The mouth of the tunnel seemed to be sucking him towards it but then, as though she feared a trap there, the lioness twisted away. The surface was stone setts, as wet and slippery as the deck of a ship, and the lioness was almost on her side as she skidded around, down Dale Street, towards the river and the Pier Head.

They crossed the Dock Road, beneath the Overhead Railway, and a little train was rattling along above them. It was all so familiar to Gerald, and should have been so reassuring and so tame – but for the menace of a maddened jackal whose poison was more virulent than rabies.

There was a ship in the river, showing lights, and the black bulk of the Liver Building was there against the night sky; and the wide, empty, plaza of the Pier Head, with just one stationary bus waiting in the Mersey mist.

Gerald's driving had become even crazier than Tim's: a mixture of bravado and fear; now showing-off how he could be master of a car in the same way that he was master of a tennis racket or a girl, and now twisting and skidding in panic, in an effort to shake-off the rabid jackal at his heels.

Foolishly, Gerald turned back, towards Tim and broadside to him; like a lioness presenting her flank to the gun. Tim saw his chance and he seemed to hear the blare of trumpets, and the stamping of a million steel-shod heels. "Sieg Heil!" he screamed, and accelerated straight into the lioness' flank.

Neither of them died instantly: neither the Blackshirt nor the Jew. Gerald was still in the driver's seat, broken and bleeding to death, when he heard Tim's voice, indistinctly, like the voice of Hitler coming out of the loudspeakers at the Nuremberg Stadium. The voice was tinny but triumphant "Your Achilles' Heel, Jew! – Achilles could handle a chariot, but you couldn't even handle a Bentley, or a sports car. Achilles died, and so did you."

The steering-wheel had gone into Tim's chest and touched his heart, and he was coughing blood. He heard sirens. They were the sirens of police-cars and of ambulances, but, what Tim heard was trumpets and a million Blackshirts singing and marching against the Jews.

About the author: -

John Rigby

The son of an expat. industrialist, John spent his early years, including the war years, in India. He returned to a catholic public-school in England. Two years National service followed, as a subaltern in the Royal Artillery, then Oxford University where he won a rugger Blue. He followed his father into industrial management for ten years before a more congenial period as a public-school master. He has always enjoyed sport: he was an England reserve at rugby and a competitive swimmer. He enjoys music, particularly opera, and good theatre.

Printed in the United Kingdom by
Lightning Source UK Ltd., Milton Keynes
136621UK00001B/31-39/P